A DREAM'S LAST EMBERS

ROMANTIC FAIRY TALES BY

NEW YORK TIMES BESTSELLING AUTHOR

SHAWNTELLE MADISON

VALKYRIE
RISING
PRESS

eBook ISBN-13: 979-8-9878431-2-3

Paperback ISBN-13: 979-8-9878431-0-9

Cover design: JV Arts

Praise for Shawntelle Madison's Fairy Tale Retellings

Loved the chemistry between the characters.

— Robyn J on *What Magic Lies Beneath*

The thing I loved about this book is the fact that the inspiration was Pinocchio. When you hear about and read retellings of fairytales, the story of Pinocchio is overlooked most of the time... The way this ended just made me want to read on, it's a very compelling book that makes you just want to keep turning the pages and then read more of this author's work! She is extremely talented and I would recommend her to everyone!

— Lyn & Nino on *Crafted with a Kiss*

Also by Shawntelle Madison

Coveted Series

Collected

Coveted

Kept

Pocketed (Novella

Compelled

Cursed (Collection of Short Stories)

Flea Market Magic Series

Thrift Store Trolls

Deceptive Dime Store Demons

Thrift Store Trolls

Heroes Run in Packs Series

Hadley Werewolves

Windham Werewolves

McGinnis Werewolves

Contents

A Tiger's Rose

Crafted With A Kiss

WHAT MAGIC LIES BENEATH

1

Everbelle

A well-dressed lady—in all black, mind you—marched her way toward my bakery. It was easy to spot customers through my window. They all approached in a similar manner, their gazes focused on my front door. But hesitation peppered their steps. Some even passed my shop but doubled back.

Winter had come early to London, but that didn't stop the lady in black from tilting up her chin to the overcast sky. She plowed forward as the ribbons of her bonnet trailed after her like Queen Victoria's royal banners.

I sighed. For every time the bakery door opened, other secrets spilled out. And not all of them were as delightful as the nuts I sprinkled on freshly prepared mazarin pastries.

"How may I help you?" I asked her.

She'd barely crossed the threshold into the shop. "Miss Amberglass, please tell me the rumors are true."

I drew in a sharp breath—not too big since my corset wouldn't allow it—as the chill from outside swept through the store. In the kitchen in the back of the bakery, I caught the faint *clink* of saucers shifting on a shelf. The woman's attention never wavered. Good.

"Please come inside." While I washed flour off my hands at the nearby sink, I said, "Madame, I don't know what you've heard—"

"Don't turn me away." The door whispered shut and the bell jingled softly. "I hear you can pull the past into your pastries."

Another saucer clinked, reminding me my customer and I weren't the only people in this room.

The only living ones, anyway.

The woman continued. "My dearest brother, Richard, he was a talented baker like yourself. Every Christmas he used to prepare nesselrode cream." Her face brightened and tears glistened in her blue eyes. "After he passed, my siblings and I tried to replicate his efforts, but..."

While she spoke of her brother, the face of a chubby, freckled-cheek child came to mind. My brother. He had a mischievous smile and ruddy skin. The bitter smell of soot trailed after him. His name sat on my lips, but to speak it would cause a ruckus in my kitchen and frighten my poor customer.

My hand rose. She didn't need to explain any further. "Come back in two days, and you'll have Richard's nesselrode cream."

She grasped my damp hand between her gloved ones. Her gratitude sent warmth into me. With a small smile, she left the shop as another customer came inside.

"Just a moment." I dried my hands on my apron and glanced up with a smile. A man had entered my store.

A handsome one at that.

"Miss Everbelle Amberglass." He spoke as if he stated fact. "I'm Malcolm Featherton."

"What can I do for you?" Invisible hands tugged my apron closer to the counter. Closer to the man with tufts of mouse brown hair peeking from under a worn bowler hat.

Brother, why can't you be still today? I thought.

Mr. Featherton strode deeper into the shop, weaving around my bread stand. For some reason, he side-stepped an empty space. My gaze swept from his shiny shoes to his wide shoulders. His angular face resembled a cat's—symmetrical and pleasing to the eye. Mr. Featherton's nose was perfectly straight, while his full lips, which were wonderfully shaped, quirked into a grin.

Did I have a troublemaker in my midst?

"It's not what you can do for me," he said smoothly. "It's what I can do for you."

I licked my dry lips in annoyance. What he could do was march right back out the door. This wasn't the first time a man had sidled into my shop to speak lies dusted in sugar.

I opened my mouth to deliver a barbed reply, but a set of decorative china near the front window slid a few inches to the right.

Let him not see.

With a hawk's razor-sharp focus, Mr. Featherton's gaze flitted to the china.

Damn it, he saw it.

"How long have you been like this?" he asked.

"What?"

"You know very well what I'm talking about, Miss Amberglass. How long do you plan to *leave* him like this?"

The forced smile on my face keeled over and died.

"You're not making any sense," I said crisply. "Perhaps

you'd like to buy some pastries instead?" I gestured to a plate of apple turnovers. Maybe a meal would set his head straight.

To my horror, the plate moved away from my hand.

"He's rather mischievous," Mr. Featherton said with a chuckle.

"Excuse me? *He?*"

Mr. Featherton's smile widened and his gaze bore into me. "There's a man in here with us—I won't tell you much more—but I know you two are related and he cares for you."

My knees turned to ash. The floor could've opened up and swallowed me whole. Did he really know about my brother? No one had ever mentioned or seen him before.

When I'd remained silent for too long, he repeated his question. "How long?"

"Who are you?" was all I could manage to say.

"In the way you're able to re-create baked goods from your customer's deceased loved ones, I'm able to connect with ghosts directly." He took off his hat and laid it on my counter. "The ghosts in the neighborhood told me to come to your shop this morning."

I searched his face for answers. Was he speaking the truth?

"You're pale...Are you all right?" He reached across the counter for my hand but pulled back just as quickly.

I managed a nod. "So why did these...ghosts tell you to come here?"

"You've hidden away for years in your little shop, but you have unfinished business." His face hardened. "And your brother can't protect you anymore."

"Protect me? From what?"

"You must set him free and confront the evil that left him like this."

The fragile lock keeping the past safely tucked away in a pretty box weakened. I saw that horrid ramshackle house again. Recalled that foul-smelling bog. Smelled the scent of burning flesh...

I snapped, "Thank you for stopping by, Mr. Featherton. You may leave now."

He frowned. "Mark my words. Your brother will grow weaker as time passes." He plucked a card from his pocket and placed it on the counter. "Come see me tonight before midnight. You'll need the crimson key for your journey, and the full moon is the only time we can procure it."

Before he closed the door, he added, "Your brother told me you need to play with the dog more often."

What dog?

I peered in the direction he looked—the very same spot he'd sidestepped earlier.

2

Malcolm

After leaving Miss Amberglass's shop, the falling temperatures threatened to freeze my fingers. My tattered gloves were far too thin. Grumbling, I walked faster. Instead of working another day in my shoe repair shop, I'd given into my compulsion to help again. Based on the growing scowl on the baker's heart-shaped face, she wasn't grateful either.

My stomach growled. At least she could've offered me one of those apple turnovers for my trouble. Her brother's actions showed he was eager for her to hear what I had to say—so what made her hesitate to help him?

As I hurried southward, dodging coaches passing over the Tower Bridge into the St. John Horselydown district, I considered her first impression of me. When I'd walked in, she'd greeted me with a disarming smile, a friendly nod. Her shop was as tidy as she was—not a single dark brown tendril of her hair was out of place. Her white apron and dark blue dress were neat and pressed. At that moment I wasn't Malcolm Featherton, humble shoemaker, but someone worthy of a warm welcome. I'd tried to reveal the truth gently—which I rarely do to strangers—but the moment I told her to set her brother free, her dark eyebrows lowered and her hazel eyes grew cold.

What happened to her when her brother died? Did he die of unnatural causes? For all I knew, she might've killed him.

I shook my head and rubbed my hands together to draw heat. She didn't seem like the type to be a killer. Either way, I was still a stranger and Everbelle Amberglass wasn't the first person to doubt my words.

Years back, I had other names thrown in my direction: charlatan. Imposter. Swindler.

Back then I plied a profitable trade with carnivals, squeezing coin from the pockets of ladies eager to see my smile. I warned them of oncoming illnesses, philandering husbands, and lost wages. Telling them their lives would continue from one day to another was mundane—but if I supposedly revealed the secrets from the great beyond, I had them right where I wanted them.

The scar on the back of my neck itched like black ants scrambling along my skin. I'd received that little *reminder* to walk a straighter path four years ago. At the time I'd fed nonsense to a barmaid about her cheating spouse. Unbeknownst to me—or her apparently—the barmaid's husband really did jump from one woman to another faster than a flea off a mutt's backside. After this *gentleman's* wife, and I used the word gentleman loosely, left him, he came for me, cohorts in tow. They beat me to near-death and the cheating husband was so drunk, he slit the back of my neck instead of the front.

They left me bleeding on the wharf similar to the one I now passed. On that humid August night, instead of dying, my spirit drifted through a hidden part of London. A mystical underbelly the weak-minded couldn't see. Didn't want to see.

For the dead—who wished to speak to those who'd listen—roamed the streets day and night. Even worse, there were other malevolent creatures prowling about. Rapunzel the High Window Widow lurked around here. Only a fool would cross her during the evenings. The Handless Maiden hunted in Hyde Park for the devil who snipped off her hands. Any pedestrian in her path met the same fate.

I had to be careful now. Warning others and using my newfound knowledge should've filled my pockets with a shilling or two, but no reputable medium or carnival show wanted to employ me.

"*I've heard of your tricks, Mr. Featherton,*" they'd say with a sneer. "*I'd rather trust a pit of vipers.*"

So here I am, skipping honest work to do the bidding of up-right apparitions. I did the honorable thing, and whether Miss Amberglass showed up tonight or not was her decision. I'd done my part to pay for my past deeds.

The aroma wafting through the air from Angler's Pub tugged at me. I was far too hungry to ignore the siren call of fried fish and a pint of ale. Even if I had to play a hand or two of poker with the owner to earn my meal, I'd do it. I had a good chance of winning, too.

The pub's owner had crossed too many people in the past. The ghost of his long dead wife showed up like clockwork.

Without fail, she revealed every card he held in his

hands.

Everbelle

THE SUN SET and the afternoon become evening. Powdery snowdrifts formed along the streets as a blizzard swept through the city. My tiny apartment above the shop was warm, yet I couldn't shake the chill settling into my bones.

According to the clock on the far wall in my tiny flat, I had two hours left. Ever since Mr. Featherton had left my shop, my brother hadn't made his presence known.

"Are you mad at me?" I whispered. "What did I do this time?"

Nothing quivered nearby. Usually the dark red curtains rustled or I felt the whisper of a hand patting my shoulder. I waited patiently as the flames from several candles wavered, their light casting a glow on the floral wallpaper print.

My gaze swept over my precious possessions: my brand new secretary desk to my sofa covered in imported linens. The mahogany side table where my tea service sat.

Beautiful things with no one to share them with.

I didn't have a single heirloom or any portraits from long dead ancestors on my walls. In a way, my home was an empty slate waiting for new memories. I spent my spare time reading the books from my large bookcase. Tucked between the serious books, I hid away my favorite reads, the penny dreadfuls. The gothic tales, which were gaudy and printed on thin paper, wouldn't win any literature awards, but I still lined up weekly at a local book store to purchase the newest issues. Those stories provided an escape, and every night I read to my brother before bed.

"Being stubborn isn't like you." I poured myself another cup of tea. The pot, and the tea within had long gone cold, but I didn't mind. I was used to drinking alone, and the last time I had company over, my brother had frightened them away.

Ever since my parents abandoned my brother and I in the countryside at the tender age of twelve, my life had been filled with horrors, emptiness, and finally triumphs. Seven years had passed, and I'd made a life and a sizable fortune for myself in the city. I refused to go down without a fight. Which meant I needed some answers from my brother.

"That man said he could see you...Is that true?" I stood from my cream sofa and strode around the room. "Knock once for yes and twice for no."

Nothing.

Desperation flitted through me. I had to say his name.

"Hamilton? Please."

An unseen hand tugged my ear a little. Back when we were children, he'd sneak up behind me and yank on my hair or ears. Always playful, never hurtful. And if another kid tried to do the same, they met Hamilton's fury.

"*Nobody makes my sister cry,*" he'd say.

He didn't pull my hair anymore. Maybe he'd matured? These days the sensation was gentle, as if a feather brushed against my earlobe. Why didn't he tease me like he used to? How I missed our childhood and the pranks we used to play on each other.

A raw emptiness sliced through me. Tears slipped down my cheeks.

Remembering my childhood dredged up the past. And I didn't want to remember the bog witch or her house. My brother had protected me that fateful night and his actions led to his grisly death. Would going back to that house mean the same for me?

A handkerchief slipped into my hand. I wiped my tears away and murmured thanks.

The time had come for me to take care of Hamilton. I had to set him free. Even if that meant I might die or end up alone. Truly alone. Something was wrong and I had to do something about it.

THIS LATE IN THE EVENING, shadows hid too many potential dangers. According to Mr. Featherton's card, he had a shoemaker's shop on the wharf in St. John Horsely-down. When I reached 7 Queen Street, I didn't see a well-kept storefront, but a tiny shop with dirty windows.

Did he really work here?

Maybe this wasn't a good idea. I backpedaled, but stopped cold when my brother knocked on the door instead.

"Hamilton!" I hissed.

The door swung open and the warmth drew me into the single-room stop. Behind Mr. Featherton, I spied a room with a cast iron fireplace on one side and a shoe peddler's workbench on the other. In the middle of the room, a ladder probably led to his sleeping quarters.

Mr. Featherton, wearing his black wool coat, stared at me. I stared back at him.

"You came," was all he said.

I nodded. "I'm sorry for my harsh words earlier. I was scared." I took a step closer to him. "Why do you have your coat on? Your shop is comfortable."

"No need for an apology. I knew you were coming, so I

prepared for our journey."

A journey? I swallowed past the lump in my throat. "Fine then. Why don't we secure a ride out of the city to the north?"

"You won't find the bog witch's house up there." He extinguished the only source of light in the room, a simple oil lamp. "The woman you seek shifts locations every full moon."

I sighed as we ventured out into the cold. "How do you know all this?"

"The Ghostly Gossipers." He revealed a grin that made me smile in return. "Stop in any tea shop north of the river and you'll hear everything you don't *want* to hear—and more."

"And this crimson key?" I pressed.

"Through magic, the key will open a door to a location near the witch's house...if we find the key's owner: the Never Past Midnight Madame."

"Who's that?"

"An abomination," Mr. Featherton said. "A few hours before and after midnight, she rides around in a coach searching for men. The smart ones avoid her. The lecherous ones disappear and are never seen again."

A sliver of fear danced down my spine, but if I had to find this dame to help Hamilton, I'd do anything.

"And one more thing," he added. "When in doubt, never trust your senses. Use your intuition—especially with the crimson key. It controls many things."

I nodded, ready to do what had to be done.

"We have two hours to find her. So where do we go?" I asked.

He paused before speaking. "Where you'll find men seeking women."

3

Malcolm

Facing the dangers ahead left me wary, so I tried to focus on the path ahead: a narrow boulevard filled with prostitutes standing outside of popular pubs and entertainment venues. Doors swung open and closed, filling the streets with laughter, conversation, and the twang of off-key pianos.

Winter storm be damned.

Miss Amberglass peeked through a window or two as we searched for the Madame. Had she ever visited these kinds of places before? Escorting a lady through the whorehouse district bordered on impropriety. Not that I had plans to court her. The pleasant thought had crossed my mind—who wouldn't want a lady's company on a night like this one?

Suddenly, the ghost of a fisherman tumbled out of the nearest pub. A drunk ghost? How did he drink in the first place? The fisherman, wearing nothing more than a raggedy shirt and trousers, wobbled to the left. Then the right, drawing closer to her.

"Hello there, Miss," he said, his voice paper thin. "Missssss!"

"Leave her alone," I whispered.

Miss Amberglass pursed her lips at my words. "Excuse me?"

"Nothing," I replied. Speaking to the dead got me into trouble too many times.

The fisherman glanced at me, then he guffawed. "Look at you, lad. You think you got a right to walk with the likes of her?"

Indeed, he had a point. My fingers poked out through holes in my gloves while Miss Amberglass tucked her hands in rabbit-fur muffs. You couldn't miss the lopsided stitches on my wool coat compared to the fine tailoring on her velvet coat and fur-lined cape. A well-crafted, dark-blue bonnet partially obscured her face, making it difficult for me to read her expressions. Did she tolerate my presence?

"I have a pulse," I said under my breath to him. "What have you got?"

The ghost grunted, scratching his balding head. "True...watch your back, boy. The living who play with the dead never live long." With a poof, the ghost disappeared through a brick wall into the nearest pub.

At least I was rid of him. But I couldn't shake off the man's words. Once the night was over Miss Amberglass and I should never see each other again. I needed to remember my place, help her, then never see her again.

It was for the best.

Beside me Miss Amberglass hurried to keep up with my wide steps. I slowed down.

"Are you sure you want to hunt for the key?" I asked.

She gave a slight nod. Or did she shake her head?

Either way, we were now too deep into the wharfs to go back the way we came. All this snow would make it difficult to see Rapunzel the High Window Widow if she decided to sweep down to snatch us.

The frigid weather didn't deter streetwalkers from prowling the alleyways and storefronts. The oldest profession in the world functioned in droughts or blizzards.

We came upon a prostitute hiding in the shadows. She slipped into the gaslamp's light.

"Oh, well aren't you two a handsome couple?" she drawled with a thick cockney accent.

In the tight space of the narrow street, we couldn't dart of out of the way. I could barely make out the prostitute's face through her scarf and burgundy bonnet. She sauntered closer to us.

"No, no! We're not married," Miss Amberglass blurted out.

"It's not like that, huh?" The prostitute's blonde eyebrows danced. "I can pretend you two are strangers, if ya like?"

Laying a light hand on Miss Amberglass's forearm, I drew her away. By the time we passed two blocks, I realized we were running.

"Sorry about that," I murmured as I waited for her to catch her breath.

I caught an amused expression on her delicate features. Did I spy a faint sprinkle of light brown freckles on her cheeks? "That was quite hilarious, Mr. Featherton."

I laughed too, relieved she made light of the situation. Maybe she didn't mind my company after all.

As we ventured deeper into the docks, the howling

wind died away and heavy snowfall subsided. The only sounds we heard came from workers unloading goods from ships into warehouses. Men barked out orders. Whether it was day or night, the city of London never truly slept.

She ended the silence between us by asking, "You said you saw a dog in my shop?"

"Why yes, it was a brown and white corgi," I replied. "A lonely little thing, but since you can't see him, that's understandable."

She nodded. "Fascinating. How I wish I could see my brother like you do."

My heart tore a bit to hear the pain in her words. I still had family to the north in Wales, but I'd forgotten them not long after I left for better opportunities.

"It's not snowing as heavily now. Will we have to do anything to draw her out?" she asked quietly.

Good question. "Why are you whispering?"

We were very much alone, past the busy warehouses and closed up shops. Under the light of a nearby gaslamp, I paused to consider our options. I didn't want Miss Amberglass to catch a cold while searching for a woman who might never appear.

"How does she kidnap her prey?" she asked, much louder now.

"The Ghost Gossipers said she pulls up next to her victims in a closed coach."

"A shiny white coach pulled by white horses with black manes?"

"How did you know?"

Miss Amberglass pointed behind me. I pivoted on my heel to see a coach no more than a few feet away. Horrified, I stood in front of her and took in the sight before me.

What I saw was by no means a gleaming white coach.

In the front, the driver's seat was vacant. The back wheels had missing spokes. The coach's white paint was chipped here and there, revealing a black metal underneath. Blackish-green vines snaked down the sides and cracks covered the dark-tinted quarter lights. The skeletal mares pulling the coach pawed at the ground as black foam dripped from their mouths. The abhorrent stench of rotting fruit struck me and I grimaced, but Miss Amberglass stared at the coach in appreciative awe.

Were we seeing the same thing?

The door to the coach swung open. We peered into the gloom within, waiting until a decrepit hand appeared and beckoned us to come closer. A single ring with a blood-red ruby sat on the bony ring finger. The huge gem glinted under the gaslamp's glow as bits of the Madame's flaky flesh fell to the snow-covered road.

"Come here," a throaty voice rattled.

The Never Past Midnight Madame placed a single slippered foot on the step and partially emerged. And what a ghastly sight she made. A tiara of teeth adorned a balding head and ruby earrings tugged at enlarged earlobes. The Madame gestured for us to move nearer, her bony arm stretching out to reveal a white dress constructed from rags.

Hamilton's ghostly form materialized before us, pushing Miss Amberglass and me toward the wall. My gaze locked with Hamilton's. We stood at the same height, and determination flashed in the ghost's opaque eyes before he turned to march right up to the Madame. His misty form disappeared and reappeared, making him hard to follow.

"Your will is strong," the Madame said, "but not much else." With a flick of her fingers, as one would swat away a fly, she sent Hamilton into the air and over the roof across the street.

Not good.

Suddenly, my legs were moving. No matter how hard I tried to back away, I kept inching toward her. Closer and closer. My heart rocketed in my chest.

"Mr. Featherton, what are you doing?" Miss Amber-glass grasped my arm and tugged.

"Run away," I said between sealed lips. Unable to control myself, I pushed her away. She hit the brick wall and fell to the ground.

"Release me," I grunted.

"You're mine now," the Madame purred.

The door opened wider. I placed my foot on the step. *I'm a dead man.*

Everbelle

Somehow, I managed to stand again, bruised elbow and all. Not far from me, poor Mr. Featherton strained to resist climbing into the coach. I refused to watch someone else die.

I ran up to him and reached around his waist, clasped my hands together, and pulled.

Mr. Featherton reached for the handle, took another step up.

"Hamilton! Help him," I cried.

Precious seconds passed, then the impression of a hand appeared on Mr. Featherton's collar. Together we pushed him to the ground—but the open door remained. Unsure what to do, I knew I had to keep him out.

So I climbed into the coach and shut the door behind me.

A never-ending darkness threatened to steal my breath until an unearthly light appeared above my head. After closing off my only escape path, I turned to see the Never Past Midnight Madame glaring at me from the other side of the three-seater coach. White fabric covered every inch of the interior. A couple of feet separated us.

She could strike me at any moment.

Frowning, I tried to turn the doorknob and failed. The door had a lock.

The expression of distaste on her pale, flawless face grew. Her kohl-lined eyebrows drew inward and her rouged lips formed a pout. My gaze swept over her, searching for weapons. I'd been cornered before. Survivors made sure they knew what they were up against. She wore a gown made from white silk. Glass slippers peeked from under the hem. The only specks of color were her ruby earrings, a single ring on her fingers, and the crimson key around her neck.

I needed that key.

"You're not welcome here, witch," the Madame snapped, her voice rising.

"I'm not a witch." My voice didn't sound as confident as I wanted it to be. "Hamilton?"

"This is my domain, girl. I see everything." Her lips jerked into a feline grin. "You might not believe magic hasn't touched you, but it's baked into your flesh." She tilted her head as if she shared a secret. "Just like the goods you create in your shop."

My frown deepened.

She continued, her thin eyebrows rising. "Oh, I see now. You weren't born this way."

The Madame slid from the other side of the coach closer to me. I pressed myself against the far wall. The Madame's hands in her lap twitched, her claw-like fingernails flexing. Were those nails sharp enough to cut me?

Suddenly, the door shook. Seconds later, it rocked again.

Mr. Featherton and Hamilton hadn't forgotten about me.

"The moment you entered the bog witch's domain, you were *tainted*," the Madame said. "You should've died in that oven with the boy, but you're alive and he's dead now. Pity."

"Shut your foul mouth," I whispered.

The door rattled again. The coach jerked forward. We weren't moving yet, but the rising hairs on the back of my neck told me I needed to escape. Now.

While the Madame jabbered on about how she planned to roast me in *her* oven, my gaze flicked to the door then the key around her neck.

Could I use it to set me free? Only one way to find out.

I grabbed my skirt's hem. Took a deep breath. Then I kicked that horrible woman in the stomach. Taken aback, the Madame doubled over with a wheeze, her eyes wide. With a hard yank, I snatched the key from around her neck. The pearl necklace fell apart and the pearls rained to the floor. As they hit, my mouth dropped to see them turn into fingernails.

I shuddered.

Disgusting.

Hadn't Mr. Featherton warned me not to trust my senses?

Key in hand, I scrambled to the door. The key slipped in smoothly and I unlocked the door. The winter air whooshed through the space and the once bright room slipped into shadow.

Mr. Featherton grabbed my hand and we ran from the coach.

We seemed to run forever, darting around corners and avoiding snowdrifts in the streets. Sweat covered my back, and my lungs begged for a reprieve, but we didn't stop until we reached my bakery. My hands shook as I unlocked the door and relocked it to seal us inside.

The warm and quiet space should've eased my fast-beating heart, but chills continued to dance down my spine. Mr. Featherton leaned against the door and tried to catch his breath.

"Are you hurt?" he gasped.

"No, I'm fine." I wasn't fine, nor would I be for a while, but I was alive.

The doorway shuddered.

Mr. Featherton squeezed his eyes shut.

"What was that?" I whispered as shadows skirted past the shop's windows.

"They followed us. Sounds like a horse is trying to break in."

"You can't be serious!" I backed away from the door. A chill nipped my leg so I made sure to side-step that spot.

With his back pressed to hold the door, he pointed to the rear exit. "Run!"

"I'm not leaving you." I grabbed a rolling pin.

Mr. Featherton rolled his eyes. "Did you see those horses? They're going to trample us to death."

The doorframe shook. Wood groaned.

He added, "You'll get kicked—or eaten before you get a hit in."

I added a cleaver knife to my free hand.

He shook his head and frowned.

"Fine," I snapped, "but you're coming with me."

I crossed the room to the other side of the bakery, grasped the door handle—only to feel it turn in my hand. God help us, no. I pressed my shoulder to the door and held the handle tight. How had the Madame unlocked it?

We were trapped.

"Use the crimson key," he said with a groan.

Using my free hand, I fished the crimson key from my coat pocket. The key fit the shop's back door's keyhole perfectly. Blood-red light glowed from the keyhole, then shot upward around the door. My eyes widened as the sounds outside fell silent.

What kind of magic was this?

"Hurry!" I yelled.

Mr. Featherton rushed across the room as I opened the door and crossed the threshold. He followed.

The door slammed shut behind us.

4

Everbelle

We emerged into a field bathed in snow. The city was gone. I turned around to see a door to a hollowed-out shed. I couldn't discern our location. Were we close to London or far away? My nose told me I'd reached the bog witch's domain. Winter's tight grip hadn't smothered the land's stench. A heavy fog of rotten eggs and sulfur covered every surface.

I never thought I'd stand this close to my brother's grave site.

But here I was.

Mr. Featherton and I held hands again. When had I reached for him? I almost released him, but the strength in his warm palm seeped into me and my back straightened. I'd never held a man's hand before. Why did such a simple thing feel so powerful?

"You ready?" he whispered.

For some reason, my cheeks grew hot and I couldn't look into his eyes. "Not really. Is anyone ever ready to face what they fear?"

With a nod, he led us through the snow away from the shed. This time of the night, only the moon illuminated the landscape. Oaks and elms, their branches dusted in show, reached for us. The ground was uneven and we proceeded with caution. My skirt snagged on a thorn bush or two before we climbed and descended a hill leading to a lone house in a rocky field.

As we drew closer, unease clenched my stomach. A long time ago, I'd walked this same path with Hamilton. Was he still with me right now? I wanted to call for him, but didn't.

Years ago, daylight had revealed a desolate house and rock fence. At night, I could barely make out the one-and-a-half story house and outhouse beside it.

Mr. Featherton tugged my hand. I'd slowed down. My stomach formed impossible knots and a cold sweat dampened my forehead.

I swallowed deeply and picked up my pace. "Thank you, Mr. Featherton."

"I think we're past the point of politeness. Please call me Malcolm."

"Malcolm." I said the word with a smile. "You may use my name too."

He said my name softly and I wished I could hear him speak it again.

We found an opening to the stone fence and made our way up the path to the house. Every now and then, Malcolm paused to listen for danger. Was the bog witch waiting to snatch us before we entered her house?

"I thought I'd have more time before doing this," I murmured. "I don't know if I'm ready."

We'd reached the entryway now. I recall the door being ominous, tall and imposing. It was just a countryhouse door, weathered with time.

"Hamilton?" I whispered. "It's time, right?"

I felt a pat on my shoulder. He was here with us.

The knob twisted and the door to the bog witch's home opened.

WITHOUT A CANDLE TO light the way, I proceeded with caution into the witch's domain. My grip on the rolling pin tightened. If she wanted to shove me in her oven, this time I'd wallop her good.

I stepped inside, expecting the house to be warm and tidy. Hamilton had led me to this very parlor with a room filled with well-polished furniture. The sickeningly sweet scent of powdered sugar and cinnamon had wafted past my nose. My brother, whose stomach had grumbled since we woke up abandoned in the woods, had hurried inside.

Malcolm and I had no reason to hurry now. Dust and neglect coated the threadbare seats. Cobwebs dangled from the ceiling's corners.

I recalled weaving around this furniture toward the kitchen, clenching Hamilton's sweaty palm.

Malcolm and I stood in the middle of the room. We listened. The only sound was the wind whistling down the chimney to a dead fireplace. This room was empty but two doors from this room led elsewhere.

I knew where the first one went. I followed Hamilton's

footprints in the dust. The ghost directed me to the one place I didn't want to see: the kitchen. The bog witch had found us here, catching my brother in the middle of eating a pile of her cookies off the butcher's block in the center of the room. The old crone had advanced on us and Hamilton told me to hide.

So I'd hidden away in one of the oak cupboards while the witch chased after him. Dragged him to the oven and sealed him inside.

Fresh tears spilled down my cheeks. My chest grew tight as I remembered him screaming in pain.

An unseen hand wiped a path of dust off the oven door on the far side of the room. Did Hamilton want me to go there? At first I couldn't move, but as I inched closer and closer, my steps were more assured. Steady. I released the rusted lock on the oven door and swung it open.

I squeezed my eyes shut as a gentle wind from within the oven brushed against my face, enveloping me with serenity.

The familiar scent of soot and coal flowed through me. My Hamilton.

The door softly shut and I opened my eyes.

Malcolm squeezed my hand.

"He's gone," he said. "From the oven and from this world."

Time passed. I blinked. Suddenly, my body broke into sobs and Malcolm pulled me into his arms. He let me cry and I drew his strength into me—until we heard a sound through the walls.

A cup had fallen over from the room beside this one.

"What was that?" I released Malcolm and edged my way out of the kitchen. We crept through the parlor, waiting to see if we'd hear the sound again.

Then we caught a murmur. A hoarse wheeze coming

from the final doorway. Malcolm extended his hand for the rolling pin and I gave it to him. With his free hand, he slowly opened the door.

I could barely see a thing inside. Only the faint moonlight through a single window to our left. The light revealed a threadbare, mottled green rug leading to a cot up against the wall. The old crone lay in the bed, the rise and fall of her chest shallow. Her right arm dangled from the side. I caught a faint *tap, tap* as her fingertips knocked against the tea cup lying on the floor.

Malcolm strode across the room in two steps, held the rolling pin high, and then froze.

"What are you doing?" I pressed my hand against his arm to stop him from striking her. As much as I wanted—no, yearned—to lessen my pain, I wouldn't treat her the way she treated us. The muscles in his arm contracted. My grip tightened.

"No," I whispered.

The great bog witch wheezed again, her chest collapsing. She moved no more. The room fell silent.

Relief flooded my soul.

"It's time for us to leave," I said firmly.

Using the crimson key, we returned to my shop through the witch's front door.

We left without my brother.

I shouldn't have opened the bakery the next morning, but I couldn't stop moving. I hadn't slept all night and if I sat still, the emptiness overflowing in me would burst forth.

So I fired up the ovens. Shed tears as I wiped down the counters.

But I wasn't alone.

Malcolm swept and scrubbed the floors. And while I prepared the nesselrode cream for my customer, he donned his coat and used a shovel to clear a path for my customers.

I watched him through the window with a wistful smile.

Time to get to work.

As I combined the ingredients in the bowl, a gentle patience radiated through me, connecting me to Richard, my customer's brother. I could feel his steady hand while he zested the lemon and added the delicate shavings to the pot. Not too much. Not too little. Richard's smile came to mind as I combined the cream with candied peel, chestnuts, and cherries. He always lined the mold not once, but twice with oil. All these simple steps gave him joy and purpose—which he passed along to his family.

My time in that house hadn't tainted me as the Madame claimed.

I'd been given a final *gift*.

And it was time for me to find my purpose and keep on giving.

While the nesselrode cream set, I grabbed the ball of twine I used for packaging. With a grin, I tossed it into the center of the room. Waited.

To my delight, the ball rolled back.

"I'll have to give you a name someday." I returned to behind the counter as Malcolm edged toward the door.

"I guess I should get going now," he said with a small smile.

Did I say something wrong? It was nice to have someone here. "It's rather cold outside." Snow fell again. "I wouldn't want you out there," I added.

Malcolm sighed. "You don't need a man like me around for long," he murmured. "I have a past, Everbelle. Not a good one."

I made my way around the corner again. Skirted around

the middle of the room. When I stood before him, my heart beat far too fast.

His gaze intensified. I didn't dare look away.

He whispered, "I've come to care for you and I don't want—"

"—You have a present and a future, too." I reached up. Instead of patting his shoulder like my brother used to do to me, I let my hand rest there. Just long enough to convey my feelings. "What you do with it is up to you."

I hoped I'd said the right thing, but Malcolm picked up his coat. My heart fell. But then he placed the coat on the hook nearby, and rolled up his sleeves.

My heart soared.

Looked like I had an assistant for the day.

"Thank you, Ever," he said softly. No one had called me that name since I was little. Did Hamilton tell him that?

My face warmed and I hid my smile. Hopefully, my brother hadn't revealed every little morsel of my past.

I wanted to tell Mr. Featherton many secrets in the days to come.

THE END

FEAR
OF
FALLING

1

Ireti

All griffin hatchlings fly when kicked out of the nest. When my nestmates and I were ousted from our birthplace, my brother and sisters glided along the jagged cliffs.

I fell.

One moment, I slept curled up beside my slightly older sister, Olufe, and in the next, my mother's blood-red beak picked me up by the tail and hurled me out of the warmth of our feather down-filled nest. I plunged down the side of the mountain, shrieking and screaming while the other ten hatchlings soared above me. The face of the mountain rushed at me. The ice streaks and patches of evergreen trees grew larger and larger. More vivid in smoky grays and stark greens.

The sunset-tinged earth was coming at me, and there was nothing I could do, but I refused to die head-first. I twisted my torso in time. First, my right leg hit a narrow cliff. *Crunch.* Pain seized my right limb and snatched my breath. Clouded my vision in red. Rocks, snow, and branches plummeted past me. I was falling faster and faster.

Fly, Ireti, fly.

I reached out with my claws—only finding the open air—even my smaller, gold-tipped wings, which should have captured the air and lifted me toward the eternal heavens, did nothing. Up here, the air was frigid and thin—only a griffin with strong wings could take flight.

The end was coming before I'd experienced a beginning.

"All the Awosanma hatchlings are called to the Wura Peak," Mother had said to us. *"Soon all of you will go there, find your true mate, and live as intended."*

I'd never see the Wura Peak, a massive, singular mountain to the far north, often obscured with wispy clouds.

I closed my eyes.

Before I hit, something yanked hard on my leg and swung me upward. I glanced up to see Olufe. The wind screamed in my ears as we soared toward the sky.

Even as a hatchling, Olufe's golden wings, with their white tips, extended far wider than most. Her claws held me tight—almost piercing the furred flesh of my leg. My sister was a beautiful creature to behold, but no matter how hard she flapped her wings, we continued to descend. We were flying toward the east. Toward the setting sun.

"No!" I conveyed to her via *mindspeak*, the *Awosanma* tongue without sounds. "Let me go! We're going the wrong way."

She shrieked and her grip tightened to the point of pain. "No," was her only reply.

The other hatchlings continued north while a panic

squeezed my chest. I wheezed. She still wouldn't let me go. My gaze flicked to Wura Peak in the distance. My wings could never carry me there.

All the stories our mother told us about our mating grounds faded away as the mountains turned to forest-green valleys. We were going too fast. Trees, rocks, structures all bled across my field of vision. Before we hit the treetops, another griffin swooped in to slow us down. My brother, Akin, grabbed us and we slammed into the trees.

My head rammed against a tree trunk and my body flopped to the ground. As I slipped away to unconsciousness, I watched other hatchlings disappear toward Wura Mountain.

THE FOREST FLOOR was impossibly dark. Shadowy tree trunks resembled figures reaching for us. Why couldn't I see as well anymore?

I flexed my claws—only to find I now had delicate fleshy limbs. Soft skin replaced feathers and fur. I leaned my head up, only to have pain slither down my back.

"Don't move," Olufe's familiar voice said in *mindspeak.* Her weird "hand" touched my torso. "Your leg is broken."

"What's wrong with me?" I replied.

"We're *Ground-Walkers* now. Whenever the *Awosanma* are near the ground at night, we take on a cursed form." She removed leaves from my hair. "The *Ground-Walkers* cover their fragile skin with woven sheep wool and communicate using these strange mouths."

A groan floated near my left side. I craned my head to see Akin struggling upright onto two legs. He wobbled, but managed to stand.

Olufe continued—though her voice through *mindspeak* sounded constricted. "I've been here before, but only during the day." As a stronger hatchling, Olufe had practiced flight.

Now that Akin was up, the moonlight shined on his broad shoulders. So this was what a male *Ground-Walker* looked like. But there was something ethereal about his honeyed skin, his speckled hazelnut-tinted eyes, and the tight, light-brown ringlets cascading down his shoulders.

Olufe turned to Akin as she gathered a thick branch from the moss-covered ground. "Why did you catch us?"

"Because you wouldn't have survived otherwise!" he sneered. "Why did you save her, anyway?"

I flinched.

Olufe's eyes formed slits and golden eyes deepened to molten amber. "Why *shouldn't* I?"

"Look at her." He sighed. "Not everyone is meant to survive the flight...to mate."

Olufe didn't look at me, but I did. As a *Ground-Walker*, my shorter limbs were thinner and less muscled than theirs.

My sister gathered two more branches and vines from the nearby trees. Using them, she fashioned a splint for my leg.

"This will ensure the leg heals straight," she reassured me with a smile. "Don't try to move anymore."

The side of her mouth trembled though. Her eyes blinked rapidly, and she sucked in a deep breath. My chest tightened. Olufe never showed weakness.

Akin ran his hands down his face then crouched. "Why now? Why did Mother push us to the sky so soon? We have at least until next spring."

The air down here was crisp. Wildflowers were in full bloom. Spring had arrived in the valley. We should've matured even more over the next year, but would I have grown enough for the arduous journey?

Olufe shook her head. "There were others in the air—maybe our parents read the skies wrong..." Her voice drifted to a whisper. Water fell down her cheek.

"Sister," I murmured.

"I'm fine." But she wasn't fine. Her shoulders shook, and she turned her face away.

I bit my lip hard enough to draw blood. I'd never cried before, but this action eased the tightness in my chest.

"We can't stay here," Akin finally said. "The *Ground-Walkers* live in this valley. We should return to the mountains until daylight. From there, we can try flying to Wura again."

No, he hadn't meant those words for all of us—only Olufe.

Her head whipped to him. "No—"

Sounds to the east made us freeze: tree branches breaking, heavy footsteps on the ground, *Ground-Walkers* shouting.

"C'mon!" Akin ran southwest.

I expected Olufe to follow him, but my sister hoisted me onto her back. I squeaked. The jostling was painful, but I held onto her. The sounds drew closer.

"Faster!" Akin stormed ahead, parting the underbrush.

"They're on horses, and they have dogs!" Olufe cried. "We must be swift."

My heart slammed against my chest and my headache increased ten-fold. I didn't know what a dog or horse was, but I could hear them and smell them.

Did the *Ground-Walkers* want to kill us?

The thick evergreens disappeared to reveal a clearing. We weren't alone. *Ground-Walkers* riding horses and holding strange contraptions shot nets into the sky. Two other hatchlings, too tired to fly high, fell hard. Once they hit the ground, they also assumed the *Ground-Walker* form.

One *Ground-Walker* pointed to us and shouted. Akin turned to go back the way we came, but more upright creatures approached from the west.

We were surrounded.

Akin could've run away, but he snarled at them and tried to frighten them away. The *Ground-Walkers'* nets subdued us with ease. We were dragged across the ground to metal cages and placed inside with other *Awosanma*. The two other hatchlings clung to each other.

A pair of large horses pulled our cage on a cart through the forest. Olufe continued to cradle me close while Akin brooded in the opposite corner. He stared at every movement the *Ground-Walkers* made.

The forest bled away to a rocky path with perfectly lined up evergreens along the side. At the far end of the road was a structure I'd never seen before. They'd taken rocks from the mountains and used them to construct a tall structure with holes covered in a transparent, shiny material. *Ground-Walkers* holding weapons guarded the front.

"That is their nest," Olufe whispered to me. "There are hundreds of them there. When I flew high above, I saw *Awosamna*, but none of them tried to escape to Wura for some reason." Her voice saddened as we entered through the gates and wooden doors closed behind us. "We can't stay here forever, Ireti. The mating grounds call for us. If we don't heed the call we may never leave."

2

Rhys

I'd never seen a frailer creature.

Her ratty hair—the honeyed color of the retreating sun with cinnamon streaks—partially covered a heart-shaped face with a dusting of freckles on her cheekbones. She blinked at me from within the griffin cage, revealing golden griffin eyes.

"Don't let their eyes fool you, Master Llewelyn!" Governess Gravesend hissed from behind me. She constantly reminded me of dangers any seventeen-year-old boy would already know.

I sighed. As the heir to the land of Cressedin and the coasts to the south, I'd endured yet another long day of lessons on military history. I was making my way to eat my evening meal when I saw the girl in the cage.

"Their human form is temporary," the governess added.

"Their fingernails in human form are as sharp as their beaks."

But this particular griffin, in its human form, stared at me until the larger girl, who held her, turned her head away and whispered in her ear.

Craigs, the surly stablemaster with a scowl just as deep as his receding hairline, unloaded the shapeshifting creatures from the cages into a corral.

"Why hasn't the stablemaster given them proper robes?" the governess snapped. "Their nakedness is offensive to my young master."

My hand rose to quiet her. "Stop fretting, Mrs. Gravesend."

Two stablehands eased into the cage. One was armed with a whip while the other forced the griffin children to put on the robes. One of the boys refused, even daring to bare his teeth. The whip cracked twice. I cringed as he screamed. The vicious welts on the boy's backside was a hard lesson: obey or else. The other children complied, and the tattered garments swallowed them.

"Come, it's time to eat." Mrs. Gravesend pulled me away, but as I glanced over my shoulder, the golden-eyed griffin girl with the broken leg watched me walk away.

The next morning, I had no lessons, so I snuck out of the castle to the stables and surrounding corrals. Now that the sun had risen, the griffins stalked the corral in their natural forms. The stablehands kept them collared and chained to keep them from flying away.

Without catching the eye of others, I ambled up to the fence and watched the stablemaster direct the stablehands to brand and break in the griffins. Every spring, Craigs sent out soldiers to capture young griffins and all of them ended up here. Cressedin Castle supplied the flying steeds for the entire kingdom.

"Should we put it down, sir? It's injured," one of the stablehands remarked.

What was he talking about?

I looked around the short man to see the injured griffin. The branches used to secure her broken leg fell away once she transformed into her griffin shape. Now she hobbled about, creating a pitiful sight with her shorter tail, muted brown feathers, and sickly yellow fur on her flank. Her misshapen, small wings made her unfit to carry anyone—but her hazel eyes flashed with far more determination than Craigs's.

"It's more than injured." Craigs snorted. "It's the ugliest thing I've ever seen. Even your wife doesn't look that hideous."

The stablehand threw his superior a dark look but glanced away when Craigs turned to him. No one who wanted a warm bed and daily meals disrespected the great Cressedin Griffin Master. Griffins came in wild animals, and in one season, they bent to his will.

Craigs wasn't done. "I'd rather wipe my rear end with that hide. It's useless. Go ahead and put it down."

The stablehand grabbed a club and entered the cage.

"Stop!" I scrambled to intervene. Anger settled into my stomach and propelled me closer until I stood behind Craigs.

"It's Master Llewelyn," the stablehand said.

Craigs didn't bother to face me. So be it. I faced him. "Do you take pleasure from killing them?" I asked.

"Killing *wild* animals?" Craigs's bushy black eyebrows rose.

"Wild or not, it's defenseless," I replied.

The stablemaster's brow furrowed. Then he laughed and his spittle hit my face. "Then what would you have me do, young *master*. This stronghold has withstood decades of assaults thanks to men like me. Griffin riders. You owe men like me for your wealth. As well as your pretty mud-free cloaks and blood-free blades."

Boastful bastard.

I stole a glance around me. My governess was nowhere to be seen. He'd never dare to criticize me so openly if she were here.

"Release her. Now." I extended my hand for the griffin's chain. The stablehand in the cage stiffened. Craigs and I exchanged a glare, and I refused to look away. *You're bold now, but someday, I will command this stronghold, I* thought. *When that time comes, men like you won't be welcome here.*

"Who do you think you are, boy?" He approached me, and my head barely reached his broad shoulders. "Just because you're Lord Llewelyn's son doesn't mean you command me like you do your little wet nurse."

His smirk shifted to a half-smile. "But who am I to judge a beast's worth?" He jerked his chin to the stable-hand. "Give the *precious* griffin to the boy. Let's see how long he lasts before it mars his handsome face."

The stablehand grabbed the heavy chain and handed it to me. The griffin female quickly hobbled out of the cage and pulled hard against the chain. I struggled to keep up, even failing to fall back as she sprang at me. Her crimson-colored beak sunk into my hand, but I didn't dare flinch. I should've worn gloves like the stablemaster.

While keeping a safe distance from the female, I tugged her to a pasture. Once her chain was tied to the fence, I ventured to the stables and returned with an animal medical kit.

The female continued to limp as a house cat would with an injured leg. As to how I'd get close enough to secure and wrap it again was another matter. I settled for patience, even daring to get close wearing gloves this time, but she wouldn't let me near her.

So I waited.

At the stables, I'd filled my pockets with apples. I tried to offer her one, but she nipped at me. After an hour passed, I decided to roll one of them to her. The red fruit sat next to her leg, and I rested against a nearby tree, satisfied that at least my efforts may work. The griffin flicked her head and sent the apple spinning toward my head. I ducked in time, barely able to hold in a laugh.

Her eyes formed slits. *Try giving me another apple*, her expression seemed to convey. There was a spark of rebellion in this one.

I sighed, wishing I had the same feeling. All my life I'd lived here, unable to escape my role as heir to the Cressedin throne. I had little power—what could I do to spare her life? If I set her free, how would she hunt for food or find shelter? I had to secure that broken leg.

Patience rewards the assiduous man, my father always told me. I switched tactics and spoke. "What should I call you?" I asked. "Apricot, perhaps?

Ireti

Another fruit? All morning long, the men called stablehands tossed about names like we didn't already have one. "Apple" for my sister and "Grape" for another female. How ridiculous! *Awosanma* parents named their children the moment they hatched. Each one represented what their parents expected of them.

My name meant *hope*.

"Maybe I should call you Pear," he suggested.

Things were looking too *hopeful* on my end.

I glanced at the strange *Ground-Walker*, that I now knew to be a human, and tilted my head. He wasn't like the others who whipped the griffins. He sat not far from me, tossing me delicious apples every now and then. Once in a while, he forgot about the cut on his hand and winced as he threw more food. I felt remorseful for biting him. He seemed kind, and well, apple trees didn't grow along the mountainside.

He tossed another apple. "My name is Rhys, by the way. I saw you looking at my hand. It's almost as if you understand what happened." He glanced at the bandage he wrapped around it. "I don't blame you for this."

You should, was my next thought.

Rhys continued. "You were defending yourself—which is your natural right." He sighed. "I don't understand why we need the griffins to defend Cressedin. Father said we're training five thousand men to go south to the Lucienne Isles. We need a navy—not an army of enslaved animals."

I inched forward a tad. Shook my head, flinging my errant feathers from my face. He'd cleverly tossed the fruit closer to him. It was the largest one he offered by far, practically blemish free. I could already taste the tartness on my tongue.

"Even if I name you...will you be fitted with a harness like the others?" He ran his fingers through his reddish-blonde hair. "Will the stablemaster use his whip to break your spirit?" He tilted up his chin. His soft gray eyes reflected warmth and I froze. I'd never seen such a shade of gray before. Silver-green flecks sparkled like starlight on the night of a new moon.

He flashed a boyish smile. "Do you understand what I'm saying?" He laughed. "You probably don't."

I was much closer to him now and snatched the apple. I swallowed it in one gulp. Quite tasty.

"Either way, none of you belong here," he said wistfully. "All the young griffins were flying north ...Where were they going?" He eased himself to his feet.

He approached me, bringing the pleasant scent of clean leather, but I scampered backward—until I saw his other hand held not one, but two apples.

"Can you live long enough to fly north?" He extended his hand with the fruit.

How much did he know about the *Awosanma*?

He waited again.

When sweat pooled on his brow, I went to him. When I was close enough, I gobbled up the first apple. He chuckled a bit and warmth pooled in my stomach. Why did his facial expressions fill me with such delight? Hadn't his fellow *Ground-Walkers* imprisoned me only yesterday?

"That good?" he asked, distracting me.

His empty hand floated over my head, barely brushing against my crown. "If I release the lock on your collar, you might survive the night." He stole a glance at the stables then released the lock on my collar.

He left the pasture. Was I free now?

I eased toward the rocky path leading to the woods, testing my wings with each step. They were too small. Beyond the pasture, near the stables, my brother and sister were chained to an iron fence. The stablehands already fastened saddles to their backs. My brother poked holes into his saddle with his beak, but my sister stared at me instead. She looked at me expectantly, even jerking her head toward the woods. *"Run away,"* she seemed to say. We were too far apart for *mindspeak.*

But there was nowhere for me to go. I couldn't leave her behind.

I limped after the human boy, Rhys, on his way back the stables.

My sister's words circled my head. *"We can't stay here forever, Ireti. The peaks call for us. If we don't heed the call, we'll be enslaved forever."*

I wasn't sure how I'd reach Wura Peak, but someday my siblings and I would.

3

Olufe flew long before I did. In the nest, all she had to do was extend her wings and take off. While my other nestmates fought each other over Mother's offering—a mountain goat on most days—Olufe's wings pushed them back, and she snatched the morsels Akin didn't care to eat.

Now it was a human's cupped hand that offered me food and brought buckets of water to my mouth. The older human boy, the one who called himself Rhys, visited my stable stall every day.

After a week passed, I even let him set my broken leg. Well, maybe I should admit he gave me a bucket of grubs—which equated to absolute griffin *bliss*—and I caved in as I gorged myself.

His touch was gentle as he bound my leg.

"This binding will stay no matter your size," he said.

What I preferred the most were his nighttime visits. When evening arrived and we took human form, the females stayed grouped together on one side of the barn while the males were housed on the other. Little did the humans know we chatted all night like hens using *mindspeak.*

While Akin complained about getting muzzled after he roughly bucked off Craigs, Olufe braided her thick golden hair. I loved to watch her do it. While other *Awosanma* curled up on the hay and slept, utterly exhausted from the day, my *beloved* sister hummed to herself and tied her hair in intricate plaits.

The meaning of her name, beloved, fit her well.

"What are you doing?" she asked me while her fingers worked away at her thick ringlets.

"Drawing." Over the last couple of days, I'd used both my fingernails and claws to sketch out Wura Peak on the worn stable wall.

"It's coming along nicely," she breathed.

If I closed my eyes, I pictured wisps of clouds dancing along the sheer cliffs to the snow drifts here and there. The breeze through the window tonight was warm, yet if I drifted away, I recalled the chillier temperatures up in the mountains. Taste the hint of snow in the air. I could still see the fog around the base of the mountain. Would the peak be as beautiful close up as it was from far away?

I'd give anything to be back in the nest—or at least on my way to Wura Peak.

"What are you doing?" a familiar voice asked from the locked doorway. A head appeared through the barred opening in the door.

Olufe, along with the other females, stiffened, but I

quieted them through *mindspeak*. "It's the young master. He won't hurt us."

"Drawing our homeland. Wura Peak," I replied slowly. Speaking the *Ground-Walker*'s tongue took effort, but I already understood his thoughts—all I had to do was speak what I'd already learned.

His eyes widened. "You speak...Cressedi," he marveled.

"We speak many languages," I said. Certain sounds tangled my tongue. A human mouth was a marvel indeed.

Olufe grabbed my arm and gently tugged me back.

"I can't believe griffins can speak. Wait, who's that?" he asked.

I patted Olufe's arm to reassure her. "My older sister, Olufe."

He tried to pronounce her name and did so horribly. "And what's your name?"

"Ireti," I replied, trying to hold back a smile as he did the same.

"*Ee-reh-tee*," he said slowly, catching the vowels correctly. "You have family here?" He glanced down then produced a handful of apples.

"Yes, my sister and brother. He is called Akin. The brave one." The frightened griffins refused to approach until I took the apples. I couldn't hand them out fast enough.

Once he was satisfied I was well, he gave me some pears and hurried off.

It didn't take long for Akin to convey his displeasure through *mindspeak*. "Who was the *Ground-Walker* male?"

I told them about how Rhys saved me.

"We shouldn't trust him—or his gifts," Akin replied.

"Ah," Olufe said with amusement. "Did you get pears as well?"

Silence, then a grunt of a reply. "I need to maintain my strength."

And maintain it, Akin did. Day after day, my brother was taken to the corral to be broken in, and he bucked off the stablehands with ease. Craigs was far less tolerant and Akin often returned with scars along his legs and feathers missing on his wings.

After another month, Akin fought less.

Sadly, everyone seemed that way.

Except me.

After Rhys's lessons in the morning, he came for me and took me to the castle. At first, his governess didn't approve.

"What a hideous griffin!" she remarked.

He rolled his eyes at her, but turned to me with a wink. "Oh, quiet, Mrs. Gravesend. It's no bigger than a wolfhound."

"At least a wolfhound knows how to behave in a household."

"She's housebroken—although the same can't be said for that cur Craigs."

For the next couple of weeks, I limped after Rhys. He taught me to play chess—but I wasn't too good at moving the pieces. While he read books in his study, I watched Mrs. Gravesend cross-stitch and knit. I found humans—who lacked claws to defend themselves and wings for flight—to be such frail creatures. But their hands! Those ten digits could do such wondrous things. Write on flat sheets to send messages. Sew garments to keep them warm. Cook delicious meats over a fire.

I envied them in a way, but I would have traded all my new experiences to lift my body off the ground. To soar from high up and safely reach the ground.

The spring's rains turned to a warm summer. I

continued to roam the halls as the young master's pet. I didn't like the term "pet," but Olufe pushed me to obey as well. "You'll be safer in the house, Ireti," she'd said one night to me. "Think of Akin."

We saw our brother less and less. During my time in the castle, Rhys attended many military meetings. I came along as his pet. During one of them, I learned the worst was yet to come. The strongest griffins would be sent south to the southern sea to form an offensive against Cressedin's enemies.

The army needed the griffins to cross the sea.

As the summer stretched on and I matured, I often caught Rhys staring at me from across the room while he studied. At first, I wondered if he was concerned about my leg, but as the months continued, my bone healed, though I hobbled. But he didn't stare at me while I walked.

He stared at me when I did nothing at all.

Rhys

I STARED AT HER.

I never wanted to admit it to anyone, even after she caught me a few times. After growing up with the griffins in the stables, I'd never seen them as more than wild animals to be domesticated. The griffins never appeared to communicate audibly with each other. They never interacted with humans or crafted tools. From what I could see, they had no culture to speak of.

But Ireti followed me and soaked in everything. As a smaller griffin, she was no taller than my hip, but that never stopped her from darting through the castle's corridors and exploring.

Also, Mrs. Gravesend's cross-stitching fascinated her. Once in a while, she disappeared from my side and I'd find her in my governess's quarters.

"I'm so sorry, Mrs. Gravesend," I'd say only to have my governess stiffly reply, "This is my private time, Master Lleweyn. Out the door you go. Your pet may stay."

Ireti had even won over my stubborn teacher.

During the night, I couldn't help but dream of her in human form. Ireti's human hands were small and frail, but her lips were full and my eye couldn't help but follow the new womanly curves on her body. In a few months' time, her human form blossomed from a girl into a woman's. I didn't want to ask her how griffins matured—perhaps asking such questions would reveal my feelings.

As the fall approached, I had more problems I had to face. Not only was the war with the southern islands coming to a head, but my father had plans to prepare his heir for rule.

It was time to tell Ireti what I faced.

So I led her out of the stables one night. The hints of autumn colored the leaves bright red and orange. We often walked at night and the guards never bothered us.

"You seem distant," she remarked as we strolled from the stable toward the fields. The wind played with her ringlets, and I longed to reach out and run my fingers through them. Were the curls as soft they appeared?

The half-moon hid behind an overcast sky, but I could make out her pensive face. It had been a week since I'd seen her. It was for the best.

"The frontlines to south have worsened," I began. "Many men have died."

She clasped her hands behind her back. "So I've heard."

"We will have to send men on the strongest griffins sooner rather than later. They leave at dawn."

She slowed. I continued, tossing about the number of units needed and potential losses.

"—you're rambling, Rhys. Do you have anything else to tell me?" she asked softly.

My throat tightened. "At dawn, I will be leaving, too."
She stumbled.

I kept going before I couldn't speak anymore. "I have to go—I've had to leave for a long time now, but I'd hoped to postpone this moment."

Ireti

MY HEART PLUMMETED to the ground. I never expected myself to say, "Can I go with you?"

His lower lip quivered. "I wish you could, but I already asked."

My stomach flipped. So he did want me at his side. Why did he have to leave?

Rhys tried to smile, but an awkward wall fell between us. "The hallways in Dena library are far too narrow," he added.

A part of me wanted to believe I needed him to stay for survival reasons. I'd never worn as saddle, thanks to him, and I'd learned things no griffin had ever seen.

And yet—pain settled in my chest and spread until I couldn't catch my breath. I tried to stop tears from welling in my eyes, but they slipped anyway. I cared for him, but I'd never say it. "But if you go—"

"Master Llewelyn!" Governess Gravesend called out. "Where are you?"

We both turned to see Mrs. Gravesend and a stable-hand approaching. Once she reached us, her gaze flicked back and forth.

I was grateful for the darkness as my cheeks grew warm.

The older woman said, "You must rest before your journey."

He nodded. "Of course."

Our time together was over, and soon I'd have to face my life in the castle without him. In the morning, my brother would fly to the frontlines and Rhys would go to Dena in the north.

Rhys would venture off in the very direction I needed to go home.

4

Rhys

Two years later

Cressedin's stronghold hadn't changed much in the past two years. The castle's wall had yet to be breached from invaders. The pastures stretched for miles and the fields' harvests had been taken.

New griffins yanked against chains in the cages while the older griffins milled about in the corrals.

Was Ireti one of them?

During my journey to Dena two years ago, I tried not to think of her or the pleas I made to Mrs. Gravesend to watch out for her.

"Focus on your studies," my governess always wrote back. She never told me if Ireti was alive or questioned why I cared. Why *did* I care for a griffin? We could never be together. My father, who recently passed on the responsibilities over Cressedin to me, already arranged for me to marry another nobleman's daughter.

Yet, my palms were sweaty, my heart raced, and I couldn't stop smiling at the thought of seeing Ireti again. It was mid-day—she would be in her natural form somewhere —not waiting for me with the household staff outside the castle's doors.

The carriage arrived at the castle and only the staff waited.

"Where is Mrs. Gravesend?" I asked the older man who managed the staff.

"She fell a few months ago," he explained, "and she has been taking it easy ever since then."

I hurried to Mrs. Gravesend's quarters, concerned for her well-being, only to find an interesting sight. A griffin, the size of a donkey, sat next to Mrs. Gravesend's bed. Relief fell over me as my gaze swept over a startled Ireti. I reached out and ran my hand over her feathered head.

She was alive and well.

"Lord Llewelyn? Do you plan to greet me as well?" my governess asked with a chuckle.

Ireti

HE'D RETURNED.

But nothing was the same.

After he pulled back, adding distance between us, I couldn't help beaming—as much a griffin could anyway. He was taller now, with broader shoulders and lean legs. His boyish cheeks blossomed into a square jaw. When he smiled though, his gray eyes deepened to a smoky color.

Rhys greeted Mrs. Gravesend and spoke of his journey from Dena. She nodded at the appropriate moments while I ambled to stand and gather fresh water. Avian fingers didn't work as well as a human's, but over the last few months I learned how to carry bowls, offer Mrs. Gravesend water, and keep her shivering body warm during the short summer nights.

Rhys watched me pour a cup of tea with wide eyes.

"How did you?" he began.

I over-poured the tea and accidentally took a bite of the governess's scone. I wasn't that good as a griffin caretaker, but Mrs. Gravesend refused to have me sent to the stables. Using my wing for leverage, the older woman eased herself up.

"Thank you," she said as she accepted the tea and scone.

Rhys tried to intervene, but I used my rear end to bump him out of the way. He chuckled and took a seat near the fireplace. While seated, he noticed a blanket over one of the seats.

"Did you make this?" he asked, running his fingers over the crocheted blanket. "It's Wura Peak."

My stomach jumped at the name. Last summer, during the quiet nights, my clumsy hands crafted a scene that was flimsy in my mind, but still there. A single mountain surrounded by clouds and snow. I couldn't stop thinking about it, so once I had the skill, I created it.

Why did I care for this Wura Peak? I wondered at times.

"Ireti needs some fresh air. See her out, will you?" said Mrs. Gravesend with a hint of a grin.

Rhys placed the blanket on the chair and led me out of the room. I was far larger now, but living in the castle taught me the best way to avoid bumping into the furniture or snagging the tapestries on the walls.

"You look well. Your wings are larger now," he said once

we reached outside. The weather was cool, but pleasant. Winter and summer was the same to me. My fur and feathers kept me cool or warm.

I nodded in reply. During times like these, I wished he spoke *mindspeak*. I'd tell him about all the times I tried to take off—and failed. Now that my wings were bigger, I'd learned one thing. How not to fall. Falling off one cliff was enough.

Also, I had so many questions. What did he learn? What did he see?

Did he miss me?

Rhys turned to the south. I followed his gaze. A vast line of griffins was returning. Not only had Rhys come home, but the griffin army returned also.

My breath hitched in anticipation. Would Akin be among them? Last winter, Olufe told me to forget him. Once hatchlings left the nest, nestmates rarely kept up with each other. Olufe and I were different, but Akin never cared for me.

And yet I watched the griffins, with their respective riders, sweep in. They landed softly. The scars of war marred many *Awosanma*. They squawked and shrieked at each other, but none of them used *mindspeak*.

I took a step closer to the corral. Rhys followed.

"What's wrong?" he asked.

My gaze scanned the final arrivals, and I finally saw him. He had a ghastly scar along his leg and his tail was shorter. The tip of his beautiful beak was covered in iron.

"Akin!" I called out to him in *mindspeak*.

He didn't reply.

The griffins parted as I entered the corral with Rhys beside me. The men greeted their lord as I sought out my brother. Once I reached him, I greeted him too, but his gaze seemed distant. Haunted.

"Ireti," he finally said in *mindspeak*.

He didn't belong here. Neither did I, but I couldn't quite remember where else we should be.

THAT EVENING, like all of them during this past summer, was peaceful. Usually, I slept in Mrs. Gravesend's room, but this time, I asked to look after my sister. The females' stall, which used to buzz with chatter was deathly silent. Everyone was curled up on their sides sleeping.

I found my beloved sister in human-form, with her hair tangled and knotted, lying down facing the wall. We didn't speak much to each other anymore either.

"Sister," I said fondly as I lay next to her and wrapped my arms around her waist. I ran my fingers through her hair, trying my best to work through the tangles. The room was dark for a long time until the moon peeked out from under the clouds and shined dim light through a narrow window. The light glimmered on a carving on the wall. For some reason, I paused in my task and stared.

It was the mountain again. Why did I see it everywhere?

Then I recalled Olufe's smiling face.

"It's coming along nicely," she'd said two years ago.

I closed my eyes, and a place I had trouble grasping unfolded before me: wisps of clouds danced along the sheer cliffs. This place was cold year-round, but the griffins belonged there. My sister and brother should be at Wura Peak.

As I finished my sister's braids, a final plan formed in my mind.

5

Ireti

I had to escape with Olufe and Akin, but I'd need help. I didn't have many allies in the castle, but one in particular would help me without hesitation. I made my way through the castle, dodging servants carrying breakfast, to Mrs. Gravesend's room.

She recently had her morning tea, and she sat up in her bed.

"Ireti, good morning, my dear." She offered me a warm smile, and my heart hurt to think of what I had to do.

I perched next to her bed, claiming the rug the governess left for me. I'd considered all night what I needed to do next.

"What is it?" she asked me, her wrinkled face reflecting concern. "Did my Rhys say something horrible?"

I shook my head and gathered a few pieces of parchment from the governess's desk. Her bottle of ink would be too messy to use, so using my beak I gently grasped a piece of charcoal from the fireplace.

She waited patiently, watching me while I painstakingly wrote out two words: NEED HELP.

She touched the side of my face with her soft, wrinkled hand. "Take your time. Go slow. I'm not going anywhere until I understand."

A few hours later, the plan was in place. As the day stretched on into the early afternoon, my stomach formed knot after knot. Would Mrs. Gravesend's efforts work? We had to leave before sunset.

"Stop pacing and finish packing my things," the older woman chided.

Using my beak, I grabbed her garments and placed them in her travel chest. A servant would arrive soon to take them to the carriage.

My crocheted blankets were already gone. All I needed was to wait for the servant to fetch us. He arrived in due time. I helped Mrs. Gravesend to her feet and the servant eased her onto my back.

"Neither of us walk too well," she said with a chuckle.

I limped, but I'd mastered maneuvering about just fine. Soon enough, we reached the carriage. A muzzled Olufe and Akin were chained to the back of the conveyance, their wings covered with the blankets I'd sewn.

Relief filled me, but I couldn't help looking around to see if Rhys was nearby.

As if reading my thoughts, the old woman whispered, "I'll send him a letter as I promised. We don't want him involved in our deception."

I wanted to say goodbye. Two years ago he'd given me that much.

"Please hurry," Mrs. Gravesend called to the driver.

Our team of horses were just as eager as we were to depart.

A servant tied me to the back of the carriage, and we set off. Only to reach the gates and find someone waiting for us. *Craigs.*

"Where do you think you're going with Thunder?" he barked, glancing at Akin.

As a house griffin, I wouldn't be missed. Olufe worked to defend the castle, but Akin was a military animal, a trained one at that.

Olufe and I exchanged a glance. Akin's back claws gripped the soil. We were in chains. There was nothing we could do.

"Get out of my way!" Mrs. Gravesend's voice was weak, but her command carried authority. "Show him my authorization from his lordship," she told the driver.

Craigs took the papers, read it, and tossed it to the ground. "You can go, my lady, but Thunder stays."

Mrs. Gravesend turned, and her mouth formed a determined line. "Ride straight through him then!"

The driver considered the order, then flicked the reins to set the horses to a hard gallop. The carriage jolted forward, and we raced toward Craigs—only to come to a violent stop again when armed soldiers riding griffins descended and barred our path.

Craigs's smile widened. We'd failed.

"Back off, Stablemaster!" a voice bellowed from behind us. My heart tugged to see Rhys ride up to us on horseback. He dismounted and got into the carriage. "I never got a chance to say goodbye, did I, Mrs. Gravesend?"

"No, you didn't," she replied sweetly.

Was this a part of Mrs. Gravesend's plan all along?

With one gesture, the soldiers on their griffins were forced to part and allow the carriage to roll through. The sun dipped below the horizon. Our time to escape was running out.

We hurried down the stony path to the north.

ONCE NIGHT DESCENDED, we had no choice but to make camp. In our human form, we couldn't fly home. I was torn though. I never wanted to be with him for the last time like this.

Dressed in dark blue robes, Olufe and Akin sat by the fire, staring blankly at the flames. They accepted the roasted rabbit the driver offered them but didn't acknowledge anyone.

"You look lost," Rhys remarked as he sat next to me. He brushed against my arm and I still felt the warmth through my robe.

I hurt thinking we'd never sit next to each other again. "I'm thinking about the journey tomorrow morning."

"You'll be fine," he assured me.

"No, I won't." I lifted my arms weakly. "I can't fly."

He shook his head and grasped my hand. The scar from our first encounter still marred his palm. "I'm amazed you three have reached this point. You'll find a way—together."

The seriousness in his gaze made me look away. My lips tingled, and I hungered for an action I'd seen countless times in the castle yet never experienced myself.

A kiss, my heart whispered. A true sign of adoration.

"Come with me." He tugged me to stand then released my hand.

"Why?"

He laughed a bit. "I want one last walk with you."

We walked through the woods, listening to leaves rustle,

the crickets chirp, and the owls call for each other. As we strolled, his hand often brushed against mine until he grasped me. Warmth surged from my toes to my head. I wanted this feeling to last all night. For hope, my name, to mean I could feel this way again back in Wura Peak.

The night retreated as dawn approached. I didn't want to let him go. My grip tightened on his.

"What if I don't go with them?" I whispered to him.

"No," he said with a finality that shook me to my core. "You're my summer friend, and I'd like for you to be my winter wife, but you don't belong here, Ireti."

I shook my head, watching with profound sadness as the sky lightened. "Don't say that."

"The army leaves again soon, and you know what will happen to Akin." Using our clasped hands, he drew me into his arms. His breath warmed my forehead, and my heart soared higher than I ever could fly.

"Take Akin and Olufe home," he murmured. "Your sister will never leave without you. Do the same."

"Don't you want me to stay?" My voice was different. My time was running out.

"So much—but not as much as I want you to be where you were meant to be." He bent his head down and brushed his lips against mine. Our breaths intermingled, and I quivered against him.

He kissed me. I kissed him back.

But time passed, as it always did. He drew back and held my hand until my five fingers became a bird's claws. With his free hand, he stroked my hair until bird feathers took its place.

He reluctantly let me go. "Go! Show them the way home."

I circled Akin and Olufe twice, barely managing to lift

myself off the ground. My wings were too weak.

"C'mon!" I tugged at Akin's tail. "We have to escape north."

Neither of them would take off until Mrs. Gravesend waved her cane at them. "Stop this foolishness and take your sister home!"

Sensing danger, Olufe grasped me and took off for the sky. She was stronger than our arrival two years ago, but we barely cleared the trees. Akin wasn't far behind us. He ascended with ease. Olufe and I kept dipping toward the forest before Akin grabbed my other arm and soon we ascended even higher. We were heading home.

But we were going the wrong way.

"Turn left," I directed them through *mindspeak*.

"Left... " Olufe's whisper was hard to hear, but she finally spoke.

Soon, Wura Peak appeared on the horizon. It was just as I remembered, but another place and another face tugged at me from below.

"Let me go," I whispered.

Neither of them complied.

"Let me go!" I shouted.

I was never meant to see Wura Peak. I had another home already.

Olufe's head turned, and her beautiful eyes blazed with determination. "You'll fall—"

"I already fell. I fell in love." I brushed my claw against the one she used to hold me. My sister touched her beak to my temple. She released me. Akin did the same.

I fell again, soaring and gliding with confidence, but this time I knew where I needed to go.

The End

THE FAIREST OF THEM ALL

1

Whitley

"What a pitiful little millinery," my latest customer, a middle-aged woman with a reed-thin voice, blurted. "Not a single black ascot or Tudor beret in sight."

Two sets of footsteps entered my hat shop.

From my spot in the back room, embarrassment heated my cheeks, but I straightened my back. Tilted my chin upward. Clenched my skirt with one hand and my fabric shears with the other. She wouldn't be the first or the last patron to mock my designs.

Yet something about her—an ominous presence—prickled the hairs on the back of my neck. Usually, I immediately greeted my customers, but this time, my feet remained rooted to my hiding place. Mr. Chuffs, my precocious yet balding Pomeranian, feigned bravery with a flash of tiny teeth then hid behind a stack of hatboxes near me.

Even my dog thought hiding back here was a wise choice.

I dared not peek around the corner to see the woman's face, but I nevertheless caught a whiff of her horrendous perfume. The heavy, bergamot-laden scent slithered around the flowerpot hats display, jumped over the table with wide-brimmed hats, and bludgeoned the back of my head.

"Look at the subpar hat construction." She sniffed. "How is this shop two blocks from Hyde Park? I highly doubt she sold her merchandise to King Edward's court like her little sign states. What bull—"

Beeps from a Model T bounding down the cobblestone road ate away the rest of her abominable, curse-filled rant.

"This dull place cannot be the fairest of them all," she added.

Whatever did she mean by *dull*? Did she not see the eerie glow in the velvet trim on the wide-brimmed hats or the way the golden thread in the capote bonnets shimmered? One of my clients, a Miss Muffett, had stated that she favored my sunhats during her forest outings in the spring.

I glanced through the back room's doorway to see a tall woman wearing a minx stole over a teal frock coat. A matching flowerpot hat covered her gray hair. The woman glared at the bountiful white ostrich feathers poking out of a plumed hat.

"Indeed, Your Grace." Her cohort, a wasplike man wearing a wrinkled gray day suit, hovered close. "The Hammerstein Millinery down the road is far more beguiling."

She weaved around the flowerpot hats and drew closer to the back room where I stood in secret. Five steps turned to two. Her overpowering perfume practically coated my tongue with its citrus tang.

The man tsked and shook his head as his spindly fingers flicked one of my mourning hats off its perch. The hat fell to the floor with a dreadful plop. The rustle of Mr. Chuffs' trembling behind the boxes made the man pause.

"Did you hear that, Your Grace?" he whispered.

Another step and she'd see me. I held my breath.

"Let's not dawdle here any longer, Mr. Percy." Her footsteps retreated to the door. "We came to give my notice. There is no need to deliver it face to face."

"Indeed." Percy stretched out the word with an arrogant air.

The bell attached to the door jingled, and I exhaled.

Mr. Chuffs sprang from his hiding spot, raced into the shop, then gave a triumphant bark.

"That'll show 'em." I chuckled as I picked up the mourning hat. In the middle of wiping any dust off the cap, I noticed a large piece of paper attached to my store window.

Now what could that be?

I hurried out of the store. The brisk October wind rustled an errant edge of the paper, but the vibrant crimson message was all too clear.

EVICTION NOTICE

THIS SHOP, MR. HEUREUX'S FINE HATS, IS HEREBY SERVED AN EVICTION NOTICE FROM HER GRACE, THE DUCHESS OF LEINBOROUGH. PAY FIVE TIMES YOUR RENT OR VACATE IN SEVEN DAYS.

. . .

I took a step back. Maybe my eyes played a trick on me.

Did that mean my employer, Mr. Heureux, wasn't on good terms with her? I'd never seen the man's face, yet he always left the required pounds and pence on the counter for me to pay rent.

Perhaps he hadn't paid enough?

"You got the notice, too," a deep voice said behind me.

A handsome man—nearly a foot taller than me—side-stepped manure in the street to approach me. He wore a work apron over a faded cream-colored shirt and brown trousers. His shoulders were wide and his hands far too large. As Mr. Chuffs sniffed the gentleman's shoes, my gaze swept from his worn work boots to his curly black hair. He offered a small smile, revealing two dimples along his sharp cheekbones.

I sighed. "I'm absolutely perplexed as to why."

"I don't know either." The man's dark eyebrows rose and confusion touched his features. "She owns all the buildings along this road, but she chose your place and mine."

My mouth dropped open. "That is quite strange."

We stared at each other briefly before the man spoke again. "Oh, excuse my manners. I'm Carl Princeton." The wind ruffled his hair. "It's nice to meet the lady who uses my fabric for her designs."

So this was one of the mysterious suppliers I'd never met. My employment was equally as peculiar. A year ago, a matron at the boardinghouse where I used to live informed me that a courier had left me a notice to come work at the hat shop. Unexpected as the offer was, I immediately accepted the position and was left instructions: when to open, how to greet my customers, and how to add Mr. Heureux's special price tags. All those types of things. Mr. Heureux never revealed how he acquired the materials I used—only that I should promptly carry the boxes left in front of the shop inside.

The owner also never told me why my creations appeared enchanted, but that was another story.

"The pleasure is mine, Mr. Princeton." I gave him a short nod. "My name is Whitley Snowfall."

He returned the nod, and we were left with facing what had brought us together—that horrible notice.

"I didn't want to be presumptuous, but did the owner underpay?" he asked.

"Never. He gave me the rent every month on the first Friday."

His jaw twitched. "I've never had a problem with the Leinsboroughs before. Looks like we have only one recourse."

"We must have a little *chitchat* with the Duchess of Leinsborough," I whispered.

Carl

DETERMINATION FLARED in Miss Snowfall's dark blue eyes and something else brewed in her growing frown—like a storm knocking against weather-beaten shutters. Other than her growing displeasure, her outward form appeared contained. Not a single strand strayed from her upswept black hair. Her muslin dress was impeccable, perhaps boasting a steadfast disposition.

I hoped.

With a deft turn of her wrist, she returned to her shop.

She came out with her gloves and shawl. Then she locked the front door. Above the shop I observed two pairs of eyes watching us with concern. Two blonde boys. When my gaze connected with the two children, they vanished.

Miss Snowfall joined me.

"Maybe we shouldn't go see her while holding a pair of murderous-looking shears?" I pointed to her hand.

The ratlike Pomeranian at her feet barked as if in agreement.

"Good point." She gave them to me, and I slipped them into my apron pocket.

Our journey took us southward to the duchess's shop on Cromwell Road. I expected Miss Snowfall to be chatty like most of my lady customers, but she remained taciturn as she adjusted the shawl draped over her shoulders. We walked faster until we reached the finer stores that lined Claymore Road. The carriages along this road carried dignified customers wearing tailored suits and mink coats. Voluminous hats obscured many of their faces, but their perfumes saturated the air as we made our way to northward.

As a child, I'd crossed the threshold into many of these shops, where I received a piece of candy or a tap on the head from a kind shopkeeper. Now that I'd reached twenty-six years of age, I no longer had the station I'd once possessed. That was what happened to the fifth son of a Belgian duke. No property, no title, merely an education to establish a reputable trade.

Instead of becoming a merchant like my older brother, I'd escaped to London with a few coins in my pocket and an incessant desire to make my own way.

How curious that my travels brought me back here.

Finally, we reached the Leinsborough and Sons storefront.

At least no one would recognize me.

Not a single soul west of Canterbury Lane could miss the imposing structure of the Duchess of Leinsborough's frame shop. Both royalty and the gentry often boasted of purchasing her frames for their family portraits—or as kindling for their fireplace, depending on which of her underpaid workers crafted the piece.

Mainly ornate mirrors adorned her wallpapered walls, but she also sold cheaper variations—like the one I'd used to shave this morning. The less expensive mirrors filled the back of the establishment. It was a mask to put highly decorated pieces near the front to lure in customers and give off a particular air of wealth.

Miss Snowfall and I now stood before the shop's entrance. I stuffed my hands into my pockets to gather my thoughts, but she gave a glance to Mr. Chuffs then marched through the door. I gaped for a moment before the Pomeranian barked at me.

Move it, human, he seemed to say before he turned around two times then sat.

I hurried after the milliner into the store's frigid interior.

No one greeted us while we weaved our way past a wall of round mirrors to a counter with women's hand mirrors. Through the numerous reflections, I caught all aspects of Miss Snowfall's pursed lips and her soft profile.

Halfway through the shop, we paused at an interesting sight.

"The plot thickens," Miss Snowfall murmured with a raised eyebrow.

Before us stood two displays with black mourning hats. Not a single one of them was crafted with a caring hand. Even I could make out the faults, from the poorly aligned stitches to the subpar material that made me itch just gaping at it.

"Indeed," I replied.

We strolled to the rear of the store to find a thin gentleman completing a transaction with a customer.

"Please tell His Lordship he will absolutely love his new frame," the man said.

"Good day, Mr. Percy," the customer said with a nod, and departed.

Mr. Percy should've asked us if we needed help, but he gave us a single glance, sniffed, and turned to the stack of papers at the work counter.

Miss Snowfall took a step forward with a growing frown, but I intercepted to speak first. Cooler heads would prevail.

"We both received an eviction notice this morning," I said smoothly.

"And?" Mr. Percy sniffed again, this time hard enough to shuffle the marbles that made up his brain. "Was the king's English too difficult to decipher? I thought you shop folk could at *least* read and write."

This wasn't the first time a man had mocked me. When I first opened my store back in St. John Horselydown district, many questioned why I didn't work in the docks hauling goods. Why didn't someone with my strength perform manual labor instead of spending my time with bolts of cloth, needles, and thread?

I stepped forward. "We read the notice and wanted to inquire the duchess to see if any arrangements could be made to halt the eviction. Is she available?"

Mr. Percy smirked. "Her Grace is too busy with personal affairs to deal with common folk. A suggestion?

Vacate the premises and don't bother trying another day. I doubt you could afford to pay—"

"And why not?" Miss Snowfall asked.

Mr. Percy made a face as if a manure cart had rolled through. "Even if you manage to earn, steal, or grovel for the funds, your rent is impossible to pay now." He waltzed away from us, effectively ending the conversation.

With no place to go, we left to stand before the imposing shop sign. We gazed at each other, maybe hoping someone else would tell us what to do. Pedestrians passed us, each of them set on their final destination. None of them, with their finely tailored coats or high hats, would be jobless or homeless in seven days.

"Five times the amount," I said. "All the fabric in my shop and my savings could never cover the rent." I kicked a nearby rock. "I could return to St. John Horselydown and open a new place. All hope isn't lost."

Miss Snowfall stiffened and her eyes narrowed to slits. "Your odds sound far more promising, but unfortunately, mine aren't as high."

With a swirl of her skirt and Mr. Chuffs at her heels, she marched off to the west, leaving a trail of vanilla on the breeze.

2

Whitley

The wind screeched, sending a chill down my back. From the shop's back alley to the apartment above, I counted ten steps. At the beginning of my workday, I'd thundered down them, a smile on my lips and a hope hammering in my heartbeat.

Not so much now: in seven days, we must move.

I trudged up three steps until I stopped before a young woman perched on the fourth step. Her arms were folded, and her sun-kissed skin flushed red. Emmalyn's brow furrowed as I tried to dart past her.

Mr. Chuffs sniffed my feet, then he snuck around Em to hurry upstairs.

Where's the bravery I witnessed earlier?

"Where do you think you're going?" Even after arriving at the orphanage at five, Em still had the same spark in her hazel eyes. The breeze tugged at her dark brown corkscrew curls, but she ignored the errant strands to block my passage.

"I'm going home." I wanted to push past her, but I gripped the wooden handrail tighter. At sixteen, she had an air of authority that rivaled a general.

She snorted. "I'm not surprised one bit. You took one look at that eviction sign and you wandered off, didn't you?"

"No."

"What terms does that upper-class twit want?"

"More than we can afford."

"Have you even tried to earn the money?"

Her words stabbed my side, but I didn't deflect them. I stood there as unsaid words jumped between us. Past arguments where my faults were laid bare and I tried to defend them. Not so much anymore.

With pursed lips, she slipped around me, but I caught her arm. "Where are you going?"

"To do what needs to be done. There are five kids up there who have no idea what's about to happen to them."

"You'll do no such thing. The last hat you made couldn't even be called one."

"Fair enough." She sighed, perhaps recalling the misshapen monstrosity she'd called a flowerpot hat. "But what I said still stands. Time was never on our side. It took you five years to save all of us. Don't overthink this matter."

I will come back for all of you. I'll beg. I'll steal. But I will come back for you.

The promise echoed through my head.

I bit back a sigh. I'd wasted away a year after I left Saint Margaret's Children's Home. I'd wandered the city, lost in freedom and fresh air. All the while, my closest friends and I—the Rejects, as the other children called us—waited while no one adopted us.

I did fulfill my promise and adopted them, but Em had endured abuse the moment I left. Each time I came for a child, she'd pushed the younger ones forward.

"Take them," she always said. Each time the bruises switched places, but she never begged. She never wanted me to take her next.

So I accepted the words she said this morning.

"Go down to the store and try to get a hold of Mr. Heureux." She clutched my shoulder, and her face softened. "He might help us. It's his bloody store. He should take care of this."

I nodded and returned to the shop. As I'd expected, not a single thing had shifted. Though Mr. Heureux had hired me, and effectively given my family a safe place to live, I had yet to meet him. Why would an eviction notice change that? For all I knew, the man galivanted through Europe and Asia to purchase exotic goods for his businesses. I imagined a short man with a curly head of hair and a mustache, chewing on dates in Istanbul, completely oblivious to our worries.

Which meant our troubles rested on me. This was my fight.

I donned my apron and straightened my shoulders. Time to find some rich folks and offload the stock. A shadow crossed the windows in front.

I glanced up to see Mr. Princeton waiting at the door.

Carl

Miss Snowfall's mouth parted in surprise. I hadn't expected to come over so soon either, but decisions needed to be made. She hurried to the door, unlocked it, and let me inside.

"Looks like you had a delivery while we were gone." I picked up one of the larger boxes right outside the door.

Her face scrunched up. "Those only come at the beginning of every season. How peculiar."

She picked up two smaller boxes with ease. I gave a nod of approval.

"We're in peculiar times," I said. None of the boxes had labels, but the parcels carried exotic scents. One had hints of nutmeg, while another reminded me of home in Belgium. After we hauled the boxes into the shop, we stood in front of each other again.

"How may I help you, Mr. Princeton?" She moved to place one of the boxes on her work counter, but I interceded and helped her. Our bodies brushed. Her vanilla scent filled my nostrils. My heart sped up as I backed away.

"I had a similar question. Is there anything I can do to help?" I stuffed my hands into my pockets. "I took stock of my goods, and if I sell them, I can rent another place—"

"In a far less lucrative location, I guarantee," she finished.

"Unfortunately. Are you in a better position?"

She sucked in a deep breath. Many emotions flitted over her face. Despair. Resolve. Then bitterness. "No."

"I didn't want to be presumptuous, but you're welcome to join me while I search for another shopfront."

Instead of replying, she ripped off the top to the box and yanked out the contents: colorful vermillion to periwinkle bolts of silk and chiffon lay within. Those would make fine materials to craft ribbons and scarves. The container's contents seemed to sparkle under the work counter's lamp, but I had to be mistaken.

"Mr. Nemuidesu's delivery from Asia usually arrives in the summer," she whispered.

"Have you heard from the shop owner?" I asked.

"Not a peep." She opened another shipment and retrieved spools of vibrant cotton thread. "Only these things shouldn't be here. Mr. Sjenert already sent me a parcel from Norway."

"What will you do with them?"

Her reply was quick and sharp: "I'll make the hats and sell them—like I always do."

I opened my mouth to give praise, maybe even offer help, but the stark reminder of how much we needed to pay kicked my resolve off a sheer cliff.

We *both* needed fifteen pounds.

How in God's name did she believe she could earn that much in seven days? We'd need every single minute of daylight to secure another shop.

Briefly, I considered reaching out to my title-bearing cousin in York. Could I bury my pride and beg for Miss Snowfall's sake and mine? I snorted.

Returning here to reveal my ancestry and give a bailout was out of the question. That would only invite animosity. I couldn't add value to her life—or anyone's, for that matter—through money. And for some reason I wasn't sure about yet, I wanted us to be genuine acquaintances.

"I will leave you to your pursuits. Good day, Miss Snowfall." I gave her a wave, and all she did was give me a curt nod in return. We both had work to do, and it was best for me to focus on my own troubles.

3

Whitley

Six days remained. Not long into that sober morning, I discovered a note on my work counter between Mr. Nemuidesu's bolts of cloth. Mr. Chuffs paused and dropped his little red ball while I read:

Dearest Miss Snowfall,

My apologies for my late correspondence. My business dealings around the countryside have left me far too busy. I trust you will resolve the matter with the Duchess of Leinsborough accordingly. To assist you in your pursuit, I contacted an unsavory, yet affluent client. do not be fearful. They will come in two days to purchase an auto bonnet. As always, do not mark a price on this item.

Sincerely,

Mr. Heureux

Unsavory? That didn't sound good, but an opportunity was an opportunity.

I read the letter a few more times, then pressed the paper to my face. A vivid memory flashed through my mind, like every time I smelled the hints of the past he left on the parchment. Right after I left the orphanage, I always passed a bakery on the way to the pier. To earn money to eat during that bitter winter, I'd sold newspapers weaved into flowers. One customer—a short and subdued Asian gentleman in a thick overcoat—must've taken pity on me, and gave me five shillings. Far too much money. I tried to return four. With a slow chuckle, he pushed my hand away, took his sad bouquet, and walked away.

Money in hand, I bought two decadent madeleines. I'd rarely remembered that moment until today. How the buttery dough melted in my mouth. How the delicate oval shape of the pastry fit the palm of my hand.

What a wonderful day that was.

Had Mr. Heureux enjoyed a similar treat while he wrote his letter, or was this more of his strange nature at play? As much as I wanted to contemplate the mystical dealings in the store, I had a customer coming and far too little time to craft the best hat I'd ever made in my life.

These days ladies wore wide-brimmed hats with long silk or tulle scarves that covered the face and secured the garment under their chin. I had yet to ride in an automobile, but such a grand hat made a statement: the owner had money.

Using the shimmering light blue chiffon from Mr.

Nemuidesu, I used the utmost care to cut out the fabric for the bonnet. Then I sewed the bonnet's hem with Mr. Sjenert's delicate golden thread. While I toiled away, I ate the chicken soup Emmalyn had left me to eat.

Two very long days later, I completed my masterpiece. I placed it in the display and added one of Mr. Heureux's blank price tags. Golden lettering appeared on the piece of paper: 4£. My mouth fell open. If it weren't attached to my face, my lips would've tumbled to the floor.

I'd spent two days working from midnight to sunset to complete this hat, and my employer thought four pounds would be enough?

For twenty minutes I fumed, stealing glances at the pile of Mr. Heureux's price tags on the far end of the work counter. Any moment now the customer would show up and I'd be left with hefty sum pending. The chug and whine of a Model T pulling up next to the shop caught my attention. With a muffled curse, I snatched a piece of paper and scribbled a new price.

A towering lady wearing an opaque silk veil hat and forest-green riding coat entered the store. Leather boots peeked out from under her dress. I couldn't make out the features of her face, but the chill she brought into the room made me shiver. As she approached the counter, a woody yet faintly sweet scent, like plums and cinnamon, wafted from her.

"May I help you?" I crammed my nervousness into the nearest waste bin.

"I'm searching for an auto bonnet." Her voice was as deep as a grave, barely above a whisper. "A colleague recommended this establishment."

With a hint of hesitation—who wouldn't be creeped out?—I ushered her to my selection of bonnets.

Her gloved hand traveled over the pieces, briefly pausing to trace the golden stitching. "How I love this thread. Spooled on a well-made spindle, I see. Just one *prick* from one of those things can change everything."

From under her earthy odor, the stench of dead things flared. I gripped the counter but forced a full smile. What in the heavens was she talking about?

She drifted toward my latest creation but paused when her fingers ran over the eight-pound tag.

"This is lovely, but..." She put down the hat as quickly as she retrieved it.

"It's not to your taste?"

She pointed to a two-pound hat that had long sat in the case without an owner. "I'll take this one. It will make a lovely garment to wear while I conduct *business*."

What kind of business would someone conduct smelling like they'd danced in a cemetery?

I murmured thanks—not that I wasn't grateful, but a sour feeling clenched my stomach. I'd gone from earning four pounds to two. My customer had paid the amount and even added another pound for my outstanding crafts-manship.

What an ignorant fool I was.

The money weighed heavy in my palm, but I bit my tongue for my rash decision. Why hadn't I left the price tag alone? I could've had five pounds and been closer to my goal.

Because you wanted to keep your family safe, I reminded myself.

After my disturbing customer left, I perched on a chair. Mr. Chuffs jumped into my lap for snuggles and a belly rub, but my mood had plummeted. I didn't want to go upstairs. As I ate breakfast with the children, I'd told them how I couldn't wait to earn a tidy sum from my efforts.

How I'd march up those steps and give them relief.

Not so much now.

Of course, the back door to the shop opened and Emmalyn appeared. I didn't want to face them until I had a plan. In one hand, she carried a tray of food, and she used the other hand to balance one of the children on her hip. Little Macy wiggled and squirmed to escape. Her mischievous grin made me smile.

I ignored the three-year-old's outstretched arms to snatch the loaf of bread and jar of honey on the tray. If I picked up Macy, the girl would never take an afternoon nap. I didn't know how Emmalyn minded five children through the day. Maybe her drive and patience were the fuel I needed.

"You left without breaking your fast," Em grumbled. "The boys were worried about you, so I came down to see if you were alive."

I broke the loaf in half and smothered honey on my piece. Satisfied with my drowned handiwork, I ate my meal. Licked my fingers, too. Without a customer in sight, why bother with propriety?

"Down but still kicking," I said with my mouth full.

She grabbed a stool and sat beside me. Little Macy gave up her quest when I offered her a bite of the other half of bread. For a moment I rested. The warm honey filled my empty belly, but worries settled into my bones. Emmalyn used her free had to pat my back. I wasn't a child like Macy, or even school age like the four boys upstairs, but every now and then even I needed reassurance from my younger sister.

I needed a reminder that I fought for someone other than myself.

Words that needed to be said formed at the back of my throat, but I had trouble speaking as my chest tightened. Finally, I drew a deep breath and spoke. "I never apologized for making you wait so long at Saint Margaret's, did I?"

Her hand hovered between my shoulder blades. "I never needed you to say sorry."

"But I want to do it... I need to—"

"Don't do this. I made a choice, Whit." She pressed her warm palm to my shoulder. "Nobody wanted to keep those boys together. The orphanage would've separated them. Scattered them to every borough or tossed them like trash." Her voice lowered yet grew more fervent. "Sometimes the most powerful wishes are the ones you make for others instead of yourself." She sighed. "Seeing them fight and laugh and sleep next to each other was worth every second I spent there."

She patted my back again. "I don't want to hear you mention this again, Whitley. You hear?"

We sat in silence. Her words wrapped around me and hugged me tighter than any embrace.

THE BELL over the door tinkled as someone new arrived.

It was Mr. Princeton.

"Oh, you have company." His gaze flicked to Emmalyn and Macy.

"These are my sisters." Neither of them resembled me in the least bit, but I didn't care. If Mr. Princeton did, he could go on his merry way.

"Pleasure to meet you, ladies." His presence filled the space. Perhaps if he stretched out his arms, he could touch both ends.

With my meal complete, Emmalyn rose from her seat. "If you don't come up for dinner, I will bring it to you."

I smiled. "I know. You're the best, Em."

Macy yelled in protest as Emmalyn gave Mr. Princeton a friendly "Good day, sir," and left.

Carl shifted from one foot to another. "I have good news, Miss Snowfall. This morning I found a favorable corner shop." His whole handsome face lit up with excitement. "There's even a living space in the rear."

"And the neighborhood?"

"Clean and safe." He stared at me a bit before he looked away. "The rent is a bit high, but we could make an arrangement. I am one of your suppliers. Why not work together?"

"Both of us." My face grew warm at the thought. What would it be like to stand side by side with a man and work together?

Mr. Princeton continued. "The owner said he had a lot of potential interest, so he'd only hold the property for me until tomorrow at noon."

I still needed to find a place for my family, but finding work came first. "Then we should go see him tomorrow. Care for a cup of warm tea, Mr. Princeton?"

He gave me a nod, and I prepared another serving.

Right as I sat to take a sip, Mr. Chuffs approached me with a piece of paper in his mouth. Had my mischievous friend gnawed on one of the receipts I'd drafted? No, it was another letter from Mr. Heureux. I nearly dropped the teacup.

Dear Miss Snowfall,

I received a message from our customer's courier regarding the hat. She was most pleased with her purchase, but I am disappointed that you didn't heed my advice. I will give you another chance. Tomorrow afternoon, another set of disreputable clients will arrive to purchase five opulent wide-brimmed hats. If you succeed, more profits await in the coming months. I'm certain you can step up to the challenge!

Sincerely,

Mr. Heureux

Good Lord, five opulent wide-brimmed hats in a day? And who would pick them up this time?

My head swam and the porridge I'd eaten for breakfast lurched in my stomach.

"What does it say?"

Carl repeated his question, but when I didn't reply, he grasped the paper. After he read it, he stared at his cup of tea until the steam no longer rose.

"That's an impossible order." He sighed.

"Beyond impossible. I don't have enough cloth for that many hats, let alone the time."

He scanned the goods in the store. "Could you sell them ones you already have?"

"I wish. The kind of hat he's referring to requires materials I've used already."

His forehead scrunched. "I sold most of my stock, but I've got two bolts of muslin left." The concern in his eyes made my heartbeat quicken.

"I don't have enough money to pay you."

"What you can give me doesn't matter right now. What matters is you staying here. Your whole family."

"But what about the shop you mentioned?"

He stood. "We'll consider that in the morning. We need to start cutting out the patterns out as soon as possible."

His enthusiasm set my heart aflutter. "Thank you, Mr. Princeton."

He paused at the doorway. "Call me Carl."

Carl

ON MY WAY back to the shop with my bundles, I spied another set of mysterious parcels. More deliveries from suppliers? I picked up those and entered the shop to find not only Miss Snowfall, but five eager assistants.

The shop became a hive of activity from the morning into the afternoon.

I worked at the beginning of the queue to unroll the fabric and pin the patterns. Emmalyn and another boy would cut—well, they did do the cutting until Em discovered the boy's grubby hands. Then he joined the other boys to help sort the new goods into the storage room bins.

Even Mr. Chuffs did his part and kept Macy occupied while Miss Snowfall labored at the work counter to stitch the hats together.

Customers arrived and purchased goods, but with each shilling or pound earned, the crestfallen expression on Miss Snowfall's pretty face never wavered. We needed a big sale.

The afternoon stretched out, and soon our helpers disappeared. We had too many tasks to complete. Even Miss Snowfall's hands shook while she squinted to stitch together the third hat.

I grasped the needle. Her hand was cool to the touch. "Rest a bit. I can do these and apply the ribbons—but you'll have to prepare the embellishments."

Her forehead crinkled. "Yes, I must find the adornments from Signore Scontroso and Herr Blöd—as well as the ostrich feathers from Mr. Sinirli. How ever did Mr. Heureux get these shipments all the way from Italy, Germany, and Turkey here so fast?"

"Does it matter?" I took the hat and handed her a cold cup of tea and a hard scone.

She shook her head and sat. Not long into my task, I caught her light snoring and chuckled. Her features had softened, leaving her cheekbones rosy and her lips slightly parted. Her chest slowly rose and fell. Perhaps, like me, she dreamt of work—or maybe she thought of someone special?

The familiar rhythm of working a needle and thread allowed me to drift away. Working in this quiet shop with Miss Snowfall had given me something I hadn't had in a long time: contentment.

Ten minutes later, Miss Snowfall woke up with a jerk. She rubbed her eyes and peeked in the mirror customers used.

"Your hair is perfect, as usual," I whispered. "Are you ready, Miss Snowfall?"

"Yes." A blush kissed her cheeks as strength filled her voice. "No need for formalities. Please call me Whitley."

We worked side by side at the work counter. Not even a hand span separated us as she sorted out the exotic adornments: speckled glass jewelry, pendants, and pearls. She applied the feathers and adornments in becoming spots. I stitched them into place.

Our furious pace continued until darkness descended and lamps illuminated Hyde Street outside. I hadn't noticed the passage of time until I caught someone shutting the back door. A tray with two bowls, a dessert, and bread sat off to the side. Why hadn't I heard anyone enter?

Whitley continued to construct the pieces until I gently shook her shoulder.

"Let's eat, Whitley."

Her dark eyes glazed over as her pupils shrank to pinpricks. She wet her lower lip then glanced over at the meal.

"What time is it?"

"Late." I strolled past a sleeping Mr. Chuffs. His patchy belly was on full display.

Whitley took small bites of mutton stew; her gaze often flitted to the hats.

"Are you from London?" I asked to draw her into the present.

"I was born in Scotland."

"Did you come here for work?"

She slowly shook her head, and the lamp cast a warm glow on her face. "My parents died in a train accident while coming here to find work. I ended up in an orphanage. And you?"

I paused. What should I tell her? "I was born in Belgium. I came here for work, too."

"That's a long way. Not much work where you come from?"

"There's plenty—I just don't want what they have to offer." I sighed. "I've always wished for independence. Living your life through another's efforts isn't a life at all."

"Indeed." She pushed the mutton aside, then eyed the piece of mince pie. "If you don't know how to care for yourself, what can a woman or man do when life throws its worst at them?"

"They sink and drown." I would've sunk. My education and determination had carried me here. I had to do the rest.

I slid the saucer with the pie over to her.

"You are our guest, but if you don't want it…" she said.

She grasped her fork and took a bite. I softened at seeing her bliss.

"Are you sure you don't want any? Em is a fantastic cook." She appeared thoughtful. "If I earn enough money, I want to help her open a bakery."

Whitley's sister had prepared a fine meal indeed. She'd seasoned and slow-cooked the lamb well. The pie's flaky crust and sweet filling of dried fruits and spice practically called my name. But I clamped my mouth shut until Whitley rolled her eyes, picked up her knife, and sliced the pie in half.

"If you don't eat the whole thing, I will tell on you," she whispered with a grin.

After we finished our meal, we worked late into the night. By the time five hats sat on the work counter, Whitley rested against the far wall, and I stared bleary-eyed out the window. A fog had settled along the streets. As the sun rose, the clouds dissolved, leaving growing mounds of powdery white along the street.

Was that snow?

4

Whitley

I wasn't sure how long I'd dozed, but enough time had passed for my back to stiffen and my legs to go numb. I peered across my shop to find Carl staring out the window.

"What time is it?" I groaned as my hip protested from my position on the floor. "Did I sleep through opening the millinery?"

"We have worse problems than the time of day." He jerked his chin to the outdoors.

Fat and thick snowflakes fell out of the sky to join their brethren in blocking the streets. Not a single well-to-do pedestrian braved the snowdrifts.

"Snow in October..." My breath fogged the window. "I have truly wronged someone in the heavens."

Two policemen tried to plow through at snail's pace.

Another poor soul, a delivery boy carrying cake boxes, crashed face-first across the street. A delicate raspberry torte tumbled out of its box. Its gooey filling bled across the snow.

"Have faith. The weather may turn favorable."

Carl's smile should've reassured me, but as one hour passed, then two more, my faith wavered. Thick clouds obscured the sun, leaving a once vibrant street somber.

Carl donned his coat. "Let me see if I can learn when the road will be cleared." He escaped out the back door into the alley.

Time passed, and all I could do was tidy the shop. Shifting my goods a millimeter to the left or right wouldn't make them appear any more appealing. Mr. Chuffs brought me his ball again and again. Toss. Shift. Toss. Shift.

My chest grew tight as the clock on the wall reached two. Tears gathered in my eyes. I'd done everything expected of me. I'd toiled away to create this new order. I'd placed the price tags Mr. Heureux had instructed me to do.

Tomorrow, a horrible, heartless woman planned to toss my siblings into the streets. All we'd wanted—all I'd wished for—was them to feel *secure*. That old, yet familiar feeling, a hollowness in my chest and deep-set fog, smothered my senses. I was cast adrift again. Standing alone in the city with a couple pence in my pocket and no bed to rest my head.

The scrape of metal against cobblestone drew me to the window. To my surprise, I discovered Carl and the boys hard at work shoveling snow. Bit by bit, they cleared a path along the sidewalk from the end of the block to my front door.

My mouth parted and hope bubbled in my stomach. Would that be enough?

The clock ticked to two and Carl's words yesterday slammed into me: *The owner said he'd only hold the property for me until tomorrow at noon.*

Which meant he'd given up his chance at a new start.

He'd done this for me. For my family.

Once Carl and the boys reached the door, three ladies materialized behind them. Carl yanked off his cap and stepped aside.

He blurted, "Afternoon, ladies."

These highborn customers waltzed into the shop without a single snowflake on their skirts. The first young woman, by far the tallest of the three, wore a brocade-patterned, mink-lined coat. She cradled a yapping Affen-pinscher that sent poor Mr. Chuffs in a hurry into the back room. The animal appeared to be a puff of curly black fur and nothing more. The flashy black beaver hat on her head was ill-fitting, but the dramatic felt fur and silk ribbons boasted of her wealth.

Right behind her, a second woman waltzed inside. Her thick mink stole swallowed her neck and chin, revealing only her spiteful, slitted eyes from under her black lace wide-brimmed hat. Enough black feathers for flight extended upward. She strode into the shop in her moss-green tailored frock coat. The final young woman peeked from behind the second. Unlike her companions, she smiled as she took in the shop. Her lavender Tudor beret was simple, as was her thick wool capelet.

My gaze swept over them, and I considered their likes and dislikes. The first two would be trouble.

"Why did you drag me here again, Drucilla?" the second woman said.

"We're here to purchase accessories so we may secure

the affections of a *well-to-do* gentleman, Mary Millicent," Drucilla replied crisply. "Mr. Heureux told me *this* is the place to acquire the perfect match. Come along, Ursula. You dawdle too much."

I motioned for them to browse my wares. "Let me show you the selection we crafted personally for you."

Most clients loved personal attention. Ursula approached me, but Drucilla grabbed her shoulder.

"Mother told you to slow down," she said. "Always too zealous, sister."

Every single wide-brimmed hat, priced at 5£, should've caught any discerning shopper's eye. Mr. Sinirli's vibrant ostrich feathers appeared to flutter with a breeze. The golden thread from Mr. Sjenert glinted under the shop's lamps, and not a single wrinkle marred Mr. Nemuidesu's ribbons.

They'd given us the best materials to craft works of art.

"They are absolutely hideous." Drucilla frowned.

"What a waste of our time," Mary Millicent snapped.

"They're magnificent—" Ursula began, but shut her mouth when she caught her sisters' growing scowls.

What had I done wrong this time?

I picked up one of the hats and held it out. "You came all this way. Why not try it on?"

Mary Millicent exchanged one wide-brimmed hat for the other. Her sour face softened as she glanced in the mirror. "Now this is the one. A perfect fit."

Her taller sister peeked over the shoulder. She must've glimpsed her sibling's reflection, for she snatched away the hat.

"That doesn't suit you at all," Drucilla said. "It should be mine!"

Mary Millicent reached for the hat, but her sister held

her prize out of reach with one hand while her dog barked in the other. Poor Ursula stood there. Utter chaos had leapt into my establishment.

The children upstairs had better manners.

"Miss Mary Millicent, why don't you see if his hat is far more pleasing." I added with a whisper, "This one has lovely peacock feathers from Turkey."

While Drucilla admired herself in front of one mirror, Mary Millicent attached herself to another one on the opposite side of the room. That left Ursula to browse the remaining three at her leisure. She carefully considered each before she boldly said, "I'll take all three."

Not only did Drucilla and Millicent buy the hats they now wore, but two mourning hats and berets.

"Should we buy something for Cindy?" Ursula asked.

"We told you about saying the C-word," Drucilla grumbled.

Ursula rolled her eyes.

The tallest sister turned to me. "Our footman will fetch our purchases this evening."

"They will be ready before sunset." I wanted to jump with glee, but I smiled like a fool instead.

Thank goodness this was over. And that I'd never had to fight Emmalyn over such things.

She'd win in a fair fight anyway.

As my guests departed and my coffers were filled with their pounds, my joy overflowed—until I walked into the back room to find Carl holding Mr. Chuffs.

"Sounds like it went well." He grinned at me and released my fidgety pet.

"Better than well. We made thirty-five pounds today. I've never made this much money before."

"Neither have I."

Our current circumstances, or should I say Carl's, swept through the room like a bitter December breeze. I opened my mouth to offer him half, but what good would that do? Even if he used the fifteen pounds I gave him, next month's rent had to be paid.

A month from now, he would still need to find another home.

"I couldn't have done this without you," I said, knowing what had to be done. "Mr. Heureux said if I succeeded, more profits await...us."

"Us?"

I snorted. "If all these clients are as difficult as those sisters, I won't be able to do this alone. I'll need another hat maker." I fussed with my hair—then stopped when I noticed the habit. "A tailor capable of helping me meet their demands."

"Do you now?" He slipped into an easy smile.

Was that a yes? Please?

"You'll have to sleep in the storage room. Deal with my family."

"They are a handful."

"Give my dog belly rubs." Mr. Chuffs circled twice at the mention of his name. My dog sat at Carl's feet.

He's my human now, the dog seemed to declare with a bark.

I expected Carl to refuse. Hadn't he told me he wanted to find his own way? Live his life without depending on others?

"Is that it?" he said simply.

My mouth parted as I nodded. "When can you start?"

"Yesterday appeared as good a time as any, Miss Snow-fall. Yesterday."

THE END

BLOW YOUR CASTLE DOWN

Chapter 1

Cressida

Our plan is flawless, if I do say so myself.

Infiltrate the enemy Wolverine base and commandeer their mighty weapon. As much as our enemies boasted their power over their late-night bonfires, the defensive measures at their gates had gaps all over the damn place. We waltzed into their far-north fortress, skipped through their straw-thin stone walls and ambled past their snoring guards. They might as well have invited us inside for tea and biscuits.

Now we sat on the bridge of the Wolverine Horde's *greatest* achievement: their mighty steam-powered war tank called the *Lupine Leviathan*. Their leader had plastered images of the shiny, multi-level vehicle, painted in bold crimson and black colors, in every corner of my homeland, the Sunderlands. *Bend to our will and live,* every poster said.

When my people relented, we paid the price. Now my

two brothers and I controlled their monstrous tank and its powerful secret weapon, the Black Bite.

"What do you think you're doing there?" It was an older Wolverine shifter. Those damn shapeshifters didn't guard their precious things. "Are you authorized to be in there?"

My brothers glanced at me. One with alarm, and the other with an annoying trill.

"Archie, get us out of here," I said calmly. I reached for a lever on the console in front of me while Archie, my younger brother, ran through the fuel calculations and determined the best path out of here. Archie's focus drifted toward the maze of cogs and wheels before him. The soft hum of his inner workings filled my ears as I marveled at him. He stood no taller than my shoulder, but he lived after dying twice over. Now, his torso was more machine than man, with needles on the pressure gauges dancing, indicating the flow of steam through the network of pipes that comprised his circulatory system. A smile spread across my face. Banks and I had spent countless hours laboring over every detail, ensuring that every component would serve its purpose and protect Archie from harm.

After making a quick vibrato sound, Archie launched a net from the tank. Within moments, the poor guard sank under the ropes' weight.

"Why didn't you ask him to push us, Cres?" Banks asked, his huge shoulders shaking with amusement. "The Wolverines are full of themselves, I tell ya."

"Based on the current fuel supply, we can reach our intended destination at full speed," Archie supplied. He lacked a voice, so a voice synthesizer made from violin strings wheezed and sang out his words.

"We got plenty. Good." Banks chuckled and crossed his thick arms. He checked the dizzying array of dials, understanding far better how the system worked than I did. "All systems optimal," he reported.

We'd taken the ship within eighteen minutes. A feat to be celebrated. All Van Der Linds entered military training school at a young age. My brothers passed every engineering course with ease. I, on the other hand, barely passed most classes, but I had a knack for cracking codes and picking locks. There wasn't a security feature I couldn't cut through with determination and time.

"Van Der Linds are scientists. Explorers seeking fortune," my parents had touted when we were young. "You either get to the trough first, or fall behind like the runts."

With no one in our way, we left from the Wolverine fortress into the cold darkness of the forest.

"Well done, Archie," I said.

Thanks. When he didn't feel like speaking, he used sign language.

I smiled at him. A long time ago, he was so adorable. He'd had chubby cheeks and a rosy blush as he grinned with mischief. His curiosity spanned the length of the known lands in this world. Through his endeavors, he helped others conducting biomechanical research. All that ended when the wolverines attacked our home world with the *Lupine Leviathan.*

My brother barely survived and now his new body stood at my shorter height. Banks and I had managed to save him, but the wolverines succeeded in killing too many others. Over eight thousand innocent souls lost with the press of a couple buttons on this very vehicle.

Heat gathered in my chest, and I pushed away the rising anger. That feeling nourished me over the years, guided me through the training I needed for this day. I'd sacrificed everything—love, my family, my happiness—to steal the *Lupine Leviathan.*

Now I could show those wolverines my fury.

Banks glanced up from the console. "We'll reach our next target to the west in six hours."

I nodded. "We'll be ready for the beginning of the end."

Banks cocked his head to the far end of the tank's bridge. "What do we do about him?"

My gaze flicked to the tall man crouching in the corner. Handcuffs bound the Wolverine captain's hands behind him. "He's our prisoner now. It's only fair for him to watch while we blow the great Wolverine city to smithereens."

Chapter 2

Graham

Should I tell them I wasn't a crew member? Nah, I wanted to see the look on their faces when they figured out who I really was.

I flexed against the bindings on my wrists and tried to get comfortable. The bridge floor was all metal, and the designers never considered that some unlucky soul might sit and stew on the deathly cold surface.

At least it was clean.

Since those Sunds showed up with their pistols cocked and ready, I'd quickly surrendered and they tied me up. I got my calisthenics for the day following them through the *Leviathan* while they secured it.

And damn it all to the Goddess Namara's Hell, I was a few days close to freedom, too. My current employer, or should I say creditor—either way he'd all but owned me for the past few years, had contracted me to clean the *Leviathan* before the crew arrived for a tour of Wolverine Horde's enslaved countries.

The Sunds had ambushed me outside the personnel quarters, which were sparkling clean, thanks to yours truly. Yep, those pirating Sunds imprisoned the janitor. I liked to call myself a cleaning specialist first class, but the Wolverine Horde never gave the indentured help fancy titles.

Anyway, I was in the middle of sorting the captain's trousers when a Sund woman in heeled boots pointed a rifle at me. The weapon seemed far too large for her to wield, but she leveled her sharp blue eyes at me and snorted. "Look what we have here, boys. A new friend."

Her height barely met my shoulders, but the blonde woman's stance was assured. Hell, I might even say cocky. She was all belts and boots, her royal blue dress riding along feminine curves. Her heart-shaped face twitched with irritation as I gawked at her.

The thought came to mind to tackle her and see if I could wrestle the gun away, but that idea collapsed the moment a massive boar of man clamped his hand on my shoulder. "Don't even think about it, Wolverine," he grumbled.

The dark-haired man towered over my head. Of course, he had a tiny pistol, which looked like a toy compared to his meaty fist. A single silver ring dangled from his nose. More silver glinted from the golden rings on his fingers. He jerked his head to the right. "Let's go. We need to keep moving, Cressida."

The blonde woman nodded and the man drew me away from the captain's quarters. At first, I was baffled. There was little cargo on the tank. So what was worth stealing?

And what in Namara's Hell was following us down the hallway? Another member of the Sunds' party was a cybernetic humanoid, the same height as Cressida, with a tin can for a chest and spindly legs. Dirty blond locks peeked out of his cloak's hood. The man scurried along without a sound—except when the others asked him a question. Were those annoying whistles and wheezes a language?

We checked most of the nooks and crannies, finding no one as I expected. After securing the tank, they led me to the bridge, tied me up, and left me where I was currently reclining now. I could've sat there with my head down, but I had yet to rest for over thirty hours. If that man didn't stare me down once in while like he wanted to toss me overboard, I would've gotten a much-needed nap.

Cressida, who appeared to be their leader, said to the man, "Any intel on the Black Bite?"

The one they called Archie whistled three times and they turned to the larger man.

His massive mouth opened and closed, jaw cracking. Then he scratched the back of his head while glaring at me. "I don't know how these fools managed to destroy anything. There is no documentation in case of emergencies. Has the Horde ever heard of contingency plans?"

I fought back laughter—I mean, the Sunds *did* have weapons. "I don't know how the weapons system works."

"How convenient, captain," she said, still unaware I wasn't who she believed me to be. "What do you think, Banks?"

"I say we ask him about the steam system," the man said. "How do we scale up the system to make the tank fully operational?"

The gobbledygook coming out his mouth never ended. *Blah blah blah.* I was a jack of all trades kind of wolverine. Matter of fact, I was pretty handy with heating and ventilation systems, but the science-heavy stuff was over my head. What Banks should be asking me was how a bed should be made. You know, the important stuff like how to fold the corners to keep the sheet nice and taut.

"I don't know," I replied.

Banks snorted. "Cressida, he needs a reminder of how dire his circumstances will become if he doesn't comply."

"I really don't know anything," I said.

He got up. I immediately stood as he stormed my way, his footfalls heavy. There was no way I could take him on with my hands behind my back.

"*Stop*," she ordered, though her voice was soft.

The massive man halted mere inches from me. His breath was hot and foul.

"Banks, think before you rearrange his internal organs. He won't be as useful to us if you turn his spleen into pudding," she said between clenched teeth.

Banks snorted. "Useless, smelly wolverine."

Smelly? *Bah!* I sniffed myself. I smelled like the dark spice oil I rubbed through my hair. What did he know?

With a grunt, Banks returned to one of the bridge consoles. His thick fingers danced over the buttons. Was he a security officer or perhaps an engineer? Wolverines didn't intermingle with Sunds. The Horde claimed the Sunds were ignorant and lived in perpetual filth. These three didn't smell, but sure as the goddess's hairy chin, they were obstinate. Banks stabbed at a few buttons. His brow wrinkled.

"Archie, we need to feed our hungry brother," Cressida said to the cloaked figure with a sly grin.

Banks flicked a scowl at them.

A few minutes later, my jailors tugged me to the tiny mess hall. The food storage units had yet to be used much so there was plenty of food—and, boy, did Banks push the machines to their limit. He whistled while balancing plates filled with stuffed sepia-hued pheasants and pickled pears. The sentient natliss nuts tried to make a run for it, but he gobbled them up, too.

The food's heavenly scents filled the air and my stomach growled as I took in the sizzling meal. None of them asked me if I was hungry.

"What's your strategy for getting past Valencia's defenses?" Banks asked Cressida between bites.

Her chewing slowed as her face became pensive. Compared to most of my previous creditors, this pirate seemed to never speak without considering her response.

"Compared to Basgard, Valencia is covered in woodland and hill-bound farms. That kind of terrain isn't conducive for cannon fire."

Banks nodded as if they discussed trivial matters instead of mass murder. "Whether they have heavy fire artillery weapons is the problem. The hull on this bucket of bolts won't withstand a full barrage for long."

My stomach grumbled again, and I grimaced. Archie rose from his spot next to Banks. While the others chatted, the man fetched a plate of food and placed the meal before me.

I mumbled my thanks, ignoring Cressida's frown.

I had to crouch down and eat the drumsticks without the use of my hands, but at least I could eat. I filled my belly until Archie spoke to the others in that strange musical tongue of his.

"Yes, we need to arm the Black Bite before then," Cressida replied.

The coarse hairs on the back of my neck rose. Horrific images coursed through me. Fiery lights plunging through pink cloud cover to assault the farms and small cities. Mile after mile of woods would burn, killing off every creature roaming within.

These pirates are nothing more than cold-blooded killers.

I shook my head with disgust. "Did you consider there *might* be a good reason this hulk of metal doesn't have manuals?"

Cressida folded her arms. "Captain, the Horde isn't that crafty." She leaned forward. "The only thing they're good at is *killing* Sunds. I will bring your people to their knees." Her blue-eyed gaze sharpened. "You'll see."

"So that's what this is all about..." I stifled a laugh. "An eye for an eye? A tooth for a tooth?"

Her cheeks reddened, and the resolve in her gaze briefly faltered. "How about a life for a life?"

My stomach soured, then bile burned the back of my throat. Valencia didn't have many defenses, but the countryside wasn't barren. I spent a few sweat-laden years at a work camp. Most of the facilities had steam-powered farm equipment, but for every one-hundred machines, a Wolverine engineer monitored them. During the harvest season, men and women picked larmen fruit. These wolverines were *innocent*—no matter what atrocities the Horde leadership committed.

They were my people.

And with my hands tied, I couldn't do a damn thing.

Suddenly, Archie got up and left for the bridge.

"We must be close to their first set of defenses. About time," Cressida said smoothly. "I have work to do."

Cressida

If we didn't need that wolverine to uncover more of this ship's secrets, my foot would be so far down his throat you'd think I was wearing fur boots. How dare he question my motives? He was nothing more than a tool for the evil Wolverine Horde.

I marched to the bridge, ignoring the red and black propaganda posters on the walls. The Horde Overlord's hazel eyes were everywhere. I didn't bother checking to see if Archie or Banks followed. Banks had yet to complete his meal, the glutton that he was, but I caught his heavy footfalls hurrying to catch up.

By the time we reached the bridge to join Archie, I was ready to execute the second part of my plan. Months of preparation had led to this day. Soon enough, the wolverines would feel the pain I suffered. Now all I had to do was get past their defenses and activate the Black Bite—which was easier said than done. The Horde had a maze of subsystems buried within the bowels of the *Leviathan*. I scanned over the endless buttons and such on the console, but I kept coming up short. I bit my lower lip.

"Do we have control over the machine guns?" I asked.

"Affirmative," Banks replied. "By the way, I was *still* eating."

"You could've kept eating while Archie's new best friend chowed down."

"Best friend?"

"Why didn't you stop Archie from feeding that furball?" The very idea my brother would help any wolverine hurt.

Banks grumbled.

The tank jostled.

"What was that?" I asked.

"The first hit." Banks sounded impressed. Not good.

"From what?"

Bank's gaze swept over the flickering lights and gauges, then he scrambled to peer through the periscope. "Ugh! Twenty-five of them..."

"Twenty-five cannons?" I asked. Damn, I hadn't expected that many.

"Yes. And they're *all* pointed in our direction. They know we're coming."

Which meant they received a warning my people never had. There would be evacuations and less casualties. I bet the captain would be pleased.

But when I looked at him, he sat with his shoulders slumped, but the muscles along his arms were tight as if he'd fought against his cuffs.

Our gazes connected, but I looked away first. I had too much work to do.

The tank shook again and again.

"How soon until we're close enough to use the Black Bite?" I asked.

"The range is a half-mile," he replied. "We should get there an hour from now."

I gripped the console. "How many hits can the hull take before it's compromised?"

Banks spewed a bunch of numbers at Archie who gave a reply. It wasn't pretty.

I cursed.

"I'm heading to the Cannon Bay," I declared. "We need to clear a path."

At least I had access to other subsystems in the tank. The Cannon Bay was one of them. The room dwarfed the mess hall with cannons and projectile storage units. Before my engineering training this kind of place would've overwhelmed me, but my resolve burned bright and led me straight to the launch console. All the while, I tried not to think of the destruction I'd cause.

They had this coming, I reminded myself. *The Horde brought this on themselves through their treachery.*

The *Leviathan* violently lurched to the side.

I reached for a comm tube and yelled, "How bad is it out there?"

"We're drawing too much power," Banks reported back. "The propulsion pistons took a hit."

I activated the weapons system and began the process of manually feeding the black powder cartridges and fixed projectiles into the respective barrels for firing. A mechanical arm could have done this, but while under attack, I didn't want to leave anything to chance. The whole process, with the tank rocking back and forth, was precarious to say the least. Nearly a half hour later, I was drenched in sweat and soot, but I was ready.

I manned the console again and peeked through the nearby periscope. The great fortress loomed in the distance. It was beautiful. The four-story structure was much more breathtaking than my home. Pollution from the Sund factories didn't darken the clouds. Valencia's pearly white clouds parted as the townspeople evacuated the great city in the distance. Envy caught my breath. My family never had such an opportunity.

I forced myself to stand straighter. *Stay on task.* I prepared to light the many priming wires. A barrage spaced out over thirty seconds would do it.

My hand trembled as I gripped the L-shaped friction primer. After inserting the primer into the fuse hole, I'd be seconds away from firing. With one hard tug on the rope attached to the primer, there'd be one less obstacle. One less enemy in my way. And yet, all I could see was Archie's face.

His beautiful face before his mouth widened into a primal scream of pain.

No. No. No.

Archie used to say that often. In the beginning, when the surgeon said he was screaming in his head but no one could hear him cry out.

My head began to ache, yet I pushed the conflicting thought aside right as the tank took a hard hit and, *whoosh,* I was slammed headfirst to the floor. Woozy but conscious, I grabbed the console's sides, barely managing to yell, "Damn it, Banks, what's going on up there?"

"We destroyed their defenses, but there's been a breach." The comm went in and out.

Of course, they hit us. I shouldn't have hesitated. Now I yanked the first priming trigger.

A great roar filled the room. Then I pulled more triggers. Soon enough, the thunderous booms ended and there was nothing left but a dead silence. I remembered that sound all too well—after you're bombed you can only hear your heartbeat. I'd always wanted to watch the assault, but now that the time came, I was too busy running back to the bridge. I had a feeling we had a big problem. As I returned, I found Banks and Archie strapped in while our prisoner clung to another seat.

"Report in," I ordered. "What's the damage?"

Archie sang out, "Critical damage on Deck Five."

I smacked my face. Hitting the back of my head earlier wasn't as bad.

"This is their vehicle." Banks looked at me evenly. "They knew right where to hit us. They weakened the hull and now the tank is filling with exhaust fumes—"

"How long until the air won't be breathable?" I tried to sound calm.

Archie replied, "Twenty-nine minutes."

We'd exacted the first part of our revenge but took a horrible hit. "It doesn't matter. Our current trajectory will push them away from the fortress. We can still win."

"In twenty-nine, make that twenty-eight minutes, no one will be blowing up *any* castles. We'll be dead from asphyxiation," Banks griped.

I paced the bridge, a plan forming in my head. "Have you repaired something like this before, Banks?"

"No can do." He shook his head. "Most of our systems are down. When the attack took out the hull, they over-loaded the mechanical drive, the steam engine—"

"Fine, I'll fix it," I said. "Archie, I'll need you to walk me through the repair."

The wolverine's mouth dropped. "You're talking about a Malachi Air Circulation system. You don't just replace a few bolts here and there."

Of course, he'd have something to say. I ignored him and headed out. He cut me off at the door. "You can't do this alone."

"As if I'd let you help me, Captain. The minute you're released from those bonds, you'll undermine our whole operation."

He smirked. "In less than an hour, what good would that do me?"

I wanted to wipe that smirk off his face. "Well, I say you're staying—"

He turned away from me. "Banks, unlock Cargo Bay Four—"

"Hey, who are you to give orders?" I tried to add an inch to my height.

Unfortunately, Banks was already ahead of me. "We're

lucky. That cargo bay has minimal power, but you're right, the parts we need are in that section."

I scowled at both of them.

That Wolverine had the nerve to present his bound arms.

"The clock is ticking, lady," he added.

I freed him, but I wasn't nice about it on principle.

From the bridge, we dashed to the cargo bay for parts. From there, we hurried to Deck Five. The air there was so thin, almost as if we climbed through the mountains back home.

"Take it slow," the wolverine advised. "The air will only get thinner."

"Keep quiet. I know this." My frown, though, was hard to maintain as my chest grew heavier. Deck Five was full of life support machinery. I had no idea where we needed to go, so I was forced to let him take the lead as we weaved around tubes and metal support beams.

Deck Five seemed to swallow us whole. My heart began to race. What would we find? Would the repair be too much?

My mouth moved before I considered to whom I spoke, "What kind of captain knows how to repair air circulation systems? Couldn't hack it as an engineer?"

He didn't pause as he walked for a bit. Then he replied, "What kind of pirate doesn't study what they're about to commandeer? I just happen to know enough to get by."

As I followed him, I found myself straining to keep up. Each breath barely filled my lungs. I hurried to reach out and keep pace with him, closer and closer until my hand grazed his back. I caught the hard muscles along his broad shoulders. He was stronger than he appeared. I drew back as if burned.

He glanced over his shoulder. "You're breathing too fast. Slow down."

A retort circled my mouth, but I took a deep breath instead.

"I can run ahead," he offered.

"No."

"Twenty minutes, Cressida," my prisoner reminded me.

Before I could stop him, the wolverine darted ahead. He was nimble. By the time I caught up with him, he had already reached the breach point. A cluster of pipes and machinery had a jagged hole blown through it. Noxious fumes vented through the hole to the outside.

I swiftly pulled out my pistol to order him to work, but he was already shifting through the bag of parts he carried.

"How are you still so alert?" My vision briefly swam.

"I spent a year working in the Arcassian mines," he explained as he scrambled to assemble pipes. "The deeper shafts have great veins of silver. After you've toiled with little air, free air tastes like honeyed wine."

What was a captain doing working in a mine? I thought. *Guess these wolverines all had shifty pasts.*

A handheld blowtorch flared brightly in the dimly lit space. It flickered in the low oxygen room, but the shifter kept working. My vision blurred again, and I almost dropped the gun.

When I blinked, he was still furiously hammering at the pipes, and in the next moment, he had already installed his handiwork. He was fast. How much time had I lost? I still had the gun. Why hadn't he taken it from me?

"Hey, Captain?" I sounded out of breath.

"Yeah?"

"You done?"

"Don't know yet," he wheezed.

A hum vibrated through the floor into my feet. Not far from me, the wolverine slumped against the air supply system.

"Got it," he whispered.

The warm breeze against my face was heavenly. If it didn't carry a heavy odor of ozone, you would've thought it was wind off an ocean.

"Not bad. You got a name?" I was tired of calling him "Captain."

"Maybe." He relaxed and smiled, breathing more easily as he tapped the pipes and assessed his work. "If only my schoolteachers could see me now. And they said I'd never amount to anything."

I snorted. "This was no mere challenge for a captain."

"No, it wasn't, and I'm not the captain of this ship."

I forced myself to stand. My head still struggled with vertigo and gray at the edges of my sight. "But you came—"

"You assumed I was the captain, but I'm nothing more than an indentured cleaning guy."

A custodian just saved our lives? He could've sabotaged the repair and sacrificed himself. I holstered my gun. This not-a-captain wasn't going anywhere.

He said, "For the last five years, the Wolverine Horde used me as a slave to pay my family's debts."

I nodded. I enjoyed digging deep and uncovering secrets, yet with this wolverine, I realized I'd barely nicked the surface. For the first time, I took him in. He had midnight black hair, along with quiet, gray eyes. His large hands had deftly repaired the breach and his black uniform clung to his wide back down to his lean hips. My eyes followed the uniform's golden stitches to a place a refined Sund woman shouldn't look. I'd never examined these shapeshifters so closely before. A strange feeling tingled up my spine, and I jettisoned the errant thought through an escape hatch. Pleasantries would be safer. Much safer.

"So, if you're not the captain, what's your name, Wolverine?"

He considered his reply and then spoke. "I'm Graham."

Chapter 3

Graham

When my shift started this morning, I expected a dull day. This wasn't supposed to be eventful work, day in and day out, all to fulfill my debt. As I sat yet again tied up on the bridge, I considered what could've happened to me while I completed my last days.

I could've broken a leg. Maybe lose what few credits I had by gambling at the Horde saloons. Getting burned to a crisp into a steam vent shaft came to mind too. However, none of these misfortunes topped the list compared to imprisonment with Sunderland pirates.

To make things even more delightful, moments ago, I helped repair a hole in the tank they'd stolen. And based on their lovely conversation, our trajectory headed straight for the largest Wolverine Horde city.

"Cressida, most of the subsystems are operational." Banks chuckled deep in his barrel chest. "While I was repairing a couple things, I discovered how to activate the Black Bite."

Nope. My day could, in fact, get worse.

"Excellent." Cressida smiled, but her eyes appeared tired. "About time."

"Don't celebrate yet," Banks advised. "Our steam engines are at twenty percent capacity."

She hummed. "That's way too low."

"We need ninety percent minimum."

She crossed her arms and stood. "We must fix it, then, but the heat levels in that compartment are way too high. Anybody that goes in there will come out as crispy as a meat kabob."

The two exchanged a long look. Cressida's eyes formed slits while Banks avoided her stern gaze.

"We have no choice," Banks said in a lowered voice. "We've come this far. It's what we planned."

"No," she said sharply. "I need to think. There has to be another way."

Archie interrupted with a cacophony of high and low-pitched sounds.

"Not happening. The numbers don't matter. Screw logic." She sighed and slumped back into the seat. "You've sacrificed enough."

Relief coursed through me, yet a part of me felt sorry for them. They'd planned to sacrifice their lives to bring down the Horde. Taking out Valencia's defensive structures would change everything for countless indentured workers and slaves. Except now, Cressida had a change of heart.

"This is for the best, Cressida," I said. "I was born in Valencia. Not once has it fallen. It's impenetrable."

"No one *wants* your opinion, Wolverine," she grumbled.

"You might not want it, but Namara knows you should hear it," I replied.

Cressida shot to her feet again, but Banks spoke. "The way it is now, our systems are compromised. Our hull is paper-thin. Even if we have the Black Bite, we must attack from a distance."

"So that's it?" she asked him. "We'll fail if we try?"

Banks rested his large forearms on the console. "Our chances of survival are slim. But we can still try to fix the engines. After that, we can arm the cannon array again."

The two argued for a bit until the cybernetic humanoid interjected with something.

"Good idea, Archie," Banks said. "We could enter the steam engine room with high temperature suits from the engineering storage locker."

"Those clothes are useless," she replied and shook her head. "We'll die before we can finish the job."

Archie stiffly made hand signs in his sister's direction. Did he disagree with her?

She frowned at him.

Yep, apparently so.

"I *really* don't like this idea, but yes, you're the only one of us who could withstand it. All things considered, I want to see the suits first. If they don't work out, I'll consider your alternate plan," she said to him. "Got it?"

He emitted a brief affirmative trill. I think I was figuring him out.

Things seemed to settle down. The Sunds fell into silence, their choices made, but there was still a journey to reach the target. Briefly, I rested against the wall until Banks returned to the bridge in a huff.

"The Engineering Bays are secured with a hand-lock mechanism," he grumbled.

"That's impossible. I removed them," she replied.

"Not all of them." He glanced at me.

"Oh, no," I whispered. I'd helped enough already.

Cressida was already across the room. She latched onto my upper arm and pulled me to my feet. "Let's go."

"Why not just rip off his arm?" Banks asked.

"But then I couldn't fix things for you." I tried not to smirk. I failed.

Banks gave an amused chuckle as he removed my handcuffs. As Cressida and I left, he threw orders our way.

"Get those suits and get your butt back here right away. We're closing in on the city, and I'll need every minute to draw power."

Cressida marched beside me, not bothering to hold me at gunpoint. I considered slowing my pace, but that would show resistance. I had to act to end this madness, but I had to do it in a way that would take those Sunds by surprise.

I had a plan. Now to see if it'd work.

Cressida didn't say a word as we made our way to our destination. If I thought I could change her course of action, if I could convince her not to carry out her revenge, I'd try every trick I could. But how do you change the mind of someone who's willing to sacrifice their life for what they believed in?

Soon enough, we stood outside the engineering storage units. I reluctantly shoved my hand into the locking mechanism. Briefly, I closed my eyes and flexed my digits. Claws broke through my skin and my bones crackled as my body shifted into its true form. I grasped the internal lever and twisted to the right. Once done, I backed away.

The space was familiar to me, filled with storage containers, tools, and spare parts. Broken carts littered one corner. While Cressida perused the high temperature suits stored in a locker, I backed up against a desk, which I knew to be filled with papers and writing materials. I pretended to slump against the side, all the while striking a jagged sliver of metal I'd snagged from Deck Five against the desk's metal surface. Each spark bit my skin, but I kept working. Two hard scrapes, then a tiny flame ignited the papers. Thank the goddess the Horde were cheap bastards with extremely flammable taste in stationary.

"What have you done?" Cressida whispered.

Above us, sprinklers sprayed cold water over everything. As expected, the doors to the storage unit locked themselves to keep the fire from escaping.

Horde protocol dictated they wouldn't open again for at least an hour.

Chapter 4

Cressida

After Graham sealed us in into the engineering storage bay, for the first time, I honestly considered owning a wolverine pelt. Ripping it off his backside looked more and more attractive by the minute.

Once the deluge from the sprinklers ended, I advanced across the room, ready to separate his head from his body. I glanced from the burned desk to what he held. His sullen features showed no remorse.

He'd done this on purpose.

I withdrew my rifle and pointed it at his chest.

For a long time, we stared at each other, my glare bouncing off his pensive gaze. I couldn't take it anymore and turned away. Ending his life wouldn't change anything anyway. To distract myself, I inspected the door. If it had a lock mechanism, I could bypass it. However, no matter how hard I tried to crack open the door, I failed. The fire protection system was foolproof to keep clever folks like me from messing with it. We couldn't open it from inside of the room.

The comm fizzled when I tried using it to reach my brothers. I bet all the damage from enemy fire hadn't helped.

Ten minutes passed. I used a dirty work towel to dry off for the most part, but the dampness from my drenched dress left me chilled.

"You're just like our father, Cressida," Archie used to say. *"Mad one minute. Still mad in the next."*

Vengeance was a sweet nectar I sipped at my darkest moments. It kept me from drowning.

I shivered.

"Cressida, I found a shirt and trousers," Graham offered. "Do you want to change?"

I'd stared at the far wall so long I hadn't heard him moving around.

"No."

"Are you still angry?"

I rolled my eyes. "Have you given me any reason not to be?"

The wolverine was closer than I'd prefer, heat radiating from him while he clutched that stupid red shirt and black trousers. I hated those colors.

The room grew silent again, the way I preferred it, until he opened his mouth again.

"I think you're wasting a good thing." His gray eyes were kind. "When you were arming the cannons, I heard Banks talking to Archie. He said you were the best cryptographer in your class, that you saw what others couldn't see under the surface. Imagine how many people back in the Sunderlands you could've helped?"

My hands formed fists until my fingertips bit my palms.

I'd heard all of this before. And yet hearing it from that wolverine hurt.

Graham wasn't done. "I would've traded anything to get the time back. I've lost years to the Horde. I could stand here and say I'm not bitter." He laughed a bit. "I am. But I'm also ready to be free and move on."

My chest grew tight as if his words hit me harder than fists. I didn't want to cry in front of him, let alone anyone else. But there was a tenderness and a sincerity in what Graham said. Why did he have to make me feel this way? Why him of all people? He was nothing more than a wolverine shifter. I released a long sigh and found the fury to replace the sorrow.

He was closer now, and my fist found his chest. He didn't recoil, merely standing there.

"Get away from me," I bit out.

"No."

My lip trembled, and I strained to breathe. "I will get out of here."

"I know you can, Cressida."

We stared at each other again. Then Graham drew me into his arms. It was completely unexpected, and my breath caught.

What was he doing?

His large hand gently pressed the side of my head to his chest while the other ran along my back. The struggle in my stomach eased. I should've kept hitting him. He earned it with that stunt with the fire and again as he uncovered a scar I'd long kept hidden. Yet I settled into the warmth of his arms. My racing heart slowed to keep pace with his relaxed, even breaths. I closed my eyes as a feeling I'd forgotten returned: absolute relief. No one had ever given me that gift since I was younger. Once I grew up, I became

Cressida Van Der Lind, a runt better off ascending the ranks in a flight school than marrying an officer and settling down to start a family.

I wasn't worthy of affection.

Still, someone held me right now and offered me everything I thought I didn't deserve.

Graham

I'VE MADE many strange decisions. Most left me in peril. I once tried to escape that Valencian work camp in the middle of a brisk winter's night. Covered in welts and bruises from a recent beating, I squeezed through an opening in the sleeping quarter walls. For half the night, I roamed the thick forest. The barren trees' long limbs reached for me as if to pull me back where I belonged. That night I was so hungry, cold, and scared.

But not as scared as I was now holding Cressida.

Back in Valencia, I knew I'd be captured again. It was inevitable. Right now, I had a choice. For the next hour, I was trapped with her, and I chose to cross the line and find out if she'd cross it with me.

Cressida trembled against my hands. Was she cold or did she feel something else? This peculiar sensation—a flutter of lavender moths in my stomach—grew until I closed my eyes and took her in: the way her narrow shoulders relaxed, the lingering floral scent of her hair coursing through my nostrils.

A rational voice at the back of my head whispered, *"What are you doing?"*

"Something I need to do right now," was my reply.

I clutched her a bit tighter.

"You're good at this," she whispered so low I barely heard her.

"I'm out of practice." I leaned down until my nose brushed against the top of her head. "What about you?"

"Too long...and you?"

"Honestly, in a few days, I was hoping to hold someone."

She backed up a little. Had I said the wrong thing?

"Is she in Valencia?" she asked. "Your woman?"

"No. The ladies aren't interested in my charms alone."

"Ah, so you're charming now?"

"Of course. That's all I've got since I don't have credits or ancestral land for my offspring."

She didn't say anything for a bit and my mind swam with what was happening. We had nowhere to go and we'd both crossed a line with no destination except the unknown.

Time passed. Not sure how much. We'd reach Valencia soon. Cressida rested against me.

She was rather cute when she let down her guard.

When she stirred a couple minutes later, I was ready to let her go. Instead of pushing me away, she spoke. "It's crazy how you can seemingly have everything and yet still have nothing."

I wanted to agree with her, but kept quiet.

She continued. "I have eight siblings, but only one will inherit the Van Der Lind holdings."

"Your brother Banks? The big guy?"

"Oh, Banks isn't that big. Now Chester..." She spread her arms wide. "He eats my weight in food." Her words held a hint of a smile.

She went on to describe the elaborate Van Der Lind family dinners—which had all the pomp and circumstance of a state dinner—but the gluttony of a ravenous army. All the while she grinned through each detail.

Then a faint click broke her reverie. The sound banged louder and louder, the comfort that settled in my bones fading. One of her brothers must've discovered the manual release switch for the door. It had to be Banks.

As soon as the sealed door eased open, Cressida pushed away from me. I let her go without a word. The way she avoided my gaze said it all, and her rejection was just as painful. She'd needed me as much as I needed her, and still, she let me go.

Banks stormed into the room. He glanced between us. Did he notice how she tried to look at everything else *except* me? But then he stared at Cressida's boots with slumped shoulders.

"We have a problem," he reported.

"What problem?" She escaped the room—or should I say she ran away from me—and forced Banks and me to follow.

"While I was trying to figure out how to help you get out, Archie disappeared."

She groaned, her pink cheeks paling. "That tricky little snot ran the numbers again. Wasn't he supposed to wait for us to return?"

"What happened?" I asked them.

Banks' gruff voice had a dark edge. "To Archie everything is black and white. We fulfill our objective if he sacrifices himself and fixes the steam engine."

Chapter 5

Graham

Banks and I returned to the storage unit for a couple suits. He didn't ask about the fire or how his sister got trapped inside. For all I knew, if we made it out of this situation alive, I had a beating coming.

High temperature suits in hand, we met up with Cressida right outside of the short hallway leading to the engine room. The space was a compact portion of the massive, five-story tank, merely a room or two, but the shielding around the engine only suppressed so much heat. Compared to the chill in storage bay, this area was downright toasty.

I'd never stood this close before. Cleaning staff didn't toss out the trash or dust between the steam engine's turbines and pistons. Even with all my training, my mind was blown. Beyond the four heavy metal doors, there was a great machine that converted hot air into energy.

I glanced at Cressida while she donned her suit. Our gazes met, but just as quickly she glanced away. She already had sweat across her brow, and the skin along her neck glistened.

Beside me, Banks frowned. His suit went up to his chest and stopped there. Hadn't he grabbed the extra-large? Looked like he wasn't coming along.

Cressida and I hurried to set out. Pretty soon, we'd be getting a couple hits from Valencia's defense systems. To enter or leave the Valencian city, you had to get past four *Breach Resistant Iridium Clusters* walls. Each BRIC wall was a set of movable cannons made of iridium, one of the hardest substances found in Valencia. It'd be impossible for us to waltz in there easily. They'd need the Black Bite to torch the place.

We raced down the hall. Only a single light illuminated each doorway. Beyond the first gate the conditions weren't too bad. I began to sweat past the second. At the third door, I sure as Namara's Hell felt it. A painful bite crept up through my boots into the soles of my feet. Beside me, Cressida had definitely slowed. Her breath fogged over her glass visor. She took my hand so I could pull her along. I could hear her breathing too fast.

"We're not going to make it," she said no more than a few steps from the fourth gate.

The ground rumbled under our feet, but it wasn't from a hit. This was different. Every surface around us vibrated.

Over the comm, Banks said, "Archie has fixed the steam engine. Get out of there. The temperature is already rising!"

"He did it!" She clapped her hands. "Has he left yet?"

But the fourth gate didn't open.

"Archie, can you hear me?" Cressida yelled. "Don't ignore me."

"He can't hear us through the doors," I explained.

Sweat ran into my eyes while we waited. I shuffled if

only to keep moving. We couldn't stay here for much longer. Even worse, the tank was powering up the Horde's city killer. The Black Bite's concentrated beam of heat would decimate anything in its path.

Cressida made her way to the fourth gate but stumbled. I caught up with her. Through her visor, I could see her bloodshot eyes. Her hair clung to her scalp from sweat. She'd pass out before too long.

"Turn back," I barked.

"I have to save him."

I drew her back toward the third gate. She was too weak to fight me. "I'll get him."

"What? Why would you do that?"

"Because it's the right thing to do." I paused, knowing I'd made the right choice. "Trust in me."

Before she could protest, I pushed her through the third gate and made sure the door closed after her.

Time to get to work.

Graham

THE HOTTEST SUMMER on Valencia had nothing on the warmth past the fourth gate. I shifted into Wolverine form. I stood at the same height, but at least my natural form withstood the scorching waves of heat better. I gritted my teeth and plodded into the steam engine room. All the while, I told myself this jaunt would be far shorter than my longest stretch working in a mine. *One step a time, Graham.*

The whole room sparkled from gem-like stones on the walls. Great large metal pipes and valves ran from top to bottom. Eerie shadows danced as I approached the massive steam engine. It churned and hissed like a trapped animal. With each step, the foul air, composed of burning coal and oil, burned my lungs. I finally spied Archie slumped over the console at the far end of the room.

Namara, please let the Sund man be alive.

"Hey, Archie," I called. My voice was raspy. "It's Graham."

I took a wide berth around the steam engine and walked along the wall. I edged closer and closer. Almost there.

"Don't move. I'll come get you." He had to be alive. That bot made it this far after losing much of his body.

By the time I reached him, I could barely see out of my visor. My vision was spotty and my nausea rose. The very thought of puking in my suit kept my food down. Poor Archie's thin metal hands melted into the floor. I felt along his arms. There had to be a manual release to separate the hands from the body. I searched until I found release levers. The ship shook again and knocked me off-kilter, but I kept working. My diligence paid off. With another click, Archie's upper torso was freed.

Archie released a weak trill.

"You're welcome," I breathed. "Let's get you to safety."

Cressida

THE COOL AIR on my skin was welcomed, but fear tore through my stomach and raced down my spine. Shouldn't I be pleased? My brothers were alive and soon the Wolverine Horde headquarters would burn like never before.

So why did I collapse onto the bridge captain's seat with a deep regret swelling in my chest?

The tank shuddered again. I should've monitored the shields and prepared the Black Bite for firing, yet all I heard was Graham's voice. I saw his face in the back of my mind.

"You're wasting a good thing," he'd said to me.

He thought I was worthy.

He thought the same of Archie, too. My precious little brother.

"Trust in me," he'd said before he made me leave.

I cringed as I recalled what I'd seen when the fourth gate opened. Graham had risked his life to carry my brother to safety. He'd shuffled, with his back bent, as if he labored with each step across the room. He cradled Archie in his strong arms.

Now that I was back on the bridge, I could breathe a sigh of relief.

I still had a job to do. My gaze flicked to the console before me. A bright green button was ready: launch.

If I pressed that button, I'd cancel any goodwill Graham bestowed on me.

"Banks?" I asked.

He turned to me. "The Black Bite is primed and ready."

My hands shook, but my voice was steady. "Deactivate it."

"What?"

"We're done here," I said simply.

"Why?" His face fell, and I accepted his disappointment.

"I'm tired of wasting a good thing."

I waited for him to grow angry. Maybe he'd even push me out of the way and press the button himself. Instead, he looked at me in a way I hadn't expected. He gave me a long nod and turned back to the console.

"What's our new course?" he asked quietly.

"Just turn around."

Then I left the bridge.

Graham

I CAME to in the miniscule sick bay a few days later. Cressida was fast asleep in the seat next to my berth. She was snoring again.

I chuckled.

If she kept this up, I'd have to find some earplugs.

She startled awake and looked at me with a grimace. "How long have you been awake? Why didn't you wake me?"

"It was more fun watching you." My limbs felt heavy, but I wasn't in bad shape. Not far from us, Archie lay on another bed. It was good to see he'd made it.

She yawned and stretched. The shy smile she gave me made me want to sit up and draw her closer.

A silence fell around us and lasted for several minutes before she spoke again. "There's something I need to say."

I nodded.

"Back in the engineering storage locker, I pushed you away." She glanced at her hands in her lap. "I more or less made assumptions I shouldn't have." She seemed to be searching for what seemed obvious.

"And?" I prodded.

"I never considered liking a wolverine, much less wanting to be with one. I guess I'm trying to say I was scared, but I'm here now to see where things go if you want me."

My heart soared. I tried not to smile but I had a feeling I was grinning like a fool.

Her face reddened.

"So where are we?" I asked to change the subject.

She relaxed and offered me some water. "Far away from everyone."

"Why?" I expected her to chart a course back to the Sunderland Federation.

"Because in the wrong hands, this tank can be used to kill my people or wolverines. There'll be no more killing." She shrugged. "I'm tired, too."

"Okay, then. So what do you want to do?" I asked.

She slid along my body and joined me on the berth. I sighed. She lay on top of the covers, but her warmth seeped into me. With one hand, she played with the fur along my cheek. Each stroke filled me with utter bliss.

"I'm not sure," she replied. "But I'm wanted dead or alive by the Wolverine Horde."

"Me too. I missed my sign off for my cleaning detail."

"Ah, dereliction of duty." She laughed. "You are quite the rascal."

"Yup."

"Looks like we'll have to find our own ancestral lands."

"And what if we can't find anything?"

Her right eyebrow rose and her nose quivered mischievously. "Oh, we will. I have the most brilliant plan."

The End

THE TIGER'S ROSE

After three days of searching the swamps around the Everglades, I discovered the lair of the Silver Rose hidden among the intertwined mangrove trees. The thin, spindly trunks rose out of the water and obstructed jagged mounds of earth. The trees formed a wall of protection that drew me forward and beckoned me to explore. This place was far more beautiful than the noisy pedestrians and Model-Ts barreling down the rutted Miami roads.

I rather liked this place—even if I shouldn't be here.

"Don't go there," the man who'd sold me the rowboat had said. "Last I heard, some soldiers went in and never returned."

No one would stop me from going. Each day, the stakes rose as Papa weakened from his tuberculosis. To save him, I had to act sooner rather than later.

I veered around a pond. The late afternoon grew hotter instead of cooler. Sweat dampened the back of my muslin shirt down to my trousers.

Once I parted a few branches, I spied my target. A single rose, with iridescent silver petals, lay tucked away among tufts of moss and ferns. The flower resembled a queen holding court with long-claw orchids and marsh marigolds bowed before it. Each plant had a distinct scent. The orchids had subtle notes of sweet vanilla and citrus, while the marigolds were a musky blend of damp earth and hay. But the rose, oh indeed, it stood apart from the rest with hints of honey and fragrant spices. My heartbeat increased tenfold at the delightful sight.

According to Granny Adeline, Papa's mother, this part

of the swamp had been a barren wasteland of dried-up patches of mud. "Back in 1880, a circus came through here," she'd said. "A great storm arrived right behind them. It blew off the roofs, and the tide swallowed up the farmlands. A bunch of animals died, but one of them escaped—a tiger. Folks say it disappeared into the swamp. Ever since then, that area has prospered. You shouldn't go there unless you're ready to face the rose's guardian."

With the mysterious flower present, life bloomed here again. Now all I had to do was take it.

I rested my rifle against my shoulder and searched for danger. Only frog croaks and nearby herons in flight chipped away at the unsettling silence—not a single person roamed for miles around these parts.

As I crept toward where the luminescent rose perched on a smaller cliff on the hillside, a tingle tickled the back of my neck. A breeze tousled my hair, flinging chestnut strands towards my face. And yet, the wind stirred nothing within this sanctuary. Even worse, the swamp symphony ended.

Focus on the prize. My gaze locked on the fragrant petals. The scent hit my nose and left me heady. Almost there. I slung my rifle across my torso and crawled up the short, rocky ledge. The slippery rocks didn't provide the best grip. I reached and reached. My index finger almost touched the petals. I could make out the thorns along the stem. Then a growl, deep and menacing, slithered up my back. I froze. Why hadn't I seen it coming? My hunting rifle had made me too bold. I should've seen the beast coming. Something ominous—an enormous head—brushed against my right hip. Whatever it was—it had to be big. I tilted my head to peek in that direction. I caught a fleck of burnt orange and black stripes. *Oh no.* Another growl of warning came. All I had to do was reach for the gun and shoot, yet my limbs refused to move.

After sucking in two deep breaths, I prepared to twist and shoot with one arm. Then a man's hand clenched my shoulder to the left. He moved fast. Far too fast for me.

"Don't move." His grip tightened.

I glanced up and down. Where had the tiger gone? Had the beast become a man?

Somehow, my mouth formed words. "I only came for—"

"You came for something that *doesn't* belong to you."

"I need it for my father."

"This place needs it much more."

I gulped as the tall stranger pressed his chest into my back. His lips brushed my ear.

"You don't smell like the others." He nipped at my earlobe, and I stifled a shiver. "I ripped them to shreds."

My first impulse was to flinch. This man just told me he killed intruders. I'd join the fallen if I didn't kill him first. Yet a strange desire for him to move closer washed over me. I searched for the tiger again, and it was gone. This man had to be one of the creatures the elders whispered about to frighten children, a shapeshifter.

Warm breath tickled my neck as he drew his nose up my nape and buried his face in my hair. I shuddered.

"Been so long since I've encountered another one like me," he said.

Like me? Time to go. I'd fight another day with a *bigger* gun.

"If you let me go," I whispered, "I'll leave peacefully."

The hand holding my shoulder slid down my back to rest on my hip. His hard legs pressed me closer to the rock, forcing my cheek to rest against the rough stone. Briefly, I closed my eyes. This had to be a delusion—a spell cast by the shimmering rose. This lean stranger, with skin the hue of an almond, wasn't questioning me. He couldn't be real.

"You came here for me," he whispered.

White-hot shock coursed through my legs.

"I came for the rose."

He purred against my back, turning my body liquid.

"How did you learn about this place?" he asked.

I told him about Granny's tales.

"I see. She withheld some important details." He chuckled, his voice low and smooth. "Almost fifty years have passed since the first tiger arrived. Others have come, but none of them have the true lineage—like you and me."

Between clenched teeth, I murmured, "I didn't come here for you. Get your hands off me."

"So you can take the rose?" He laughed again. "Do you think I'll let you waltz out of here with it?"

My father came to mind, and I couldn't help but think about how he couldn't get up anymore. Papa needed this flower—even if Granny said otherwise.

"*Let your papa go, my sweet girl,*" she'd said. "*My son will die soon. This is how life works and there's nothing you can do about it.*"

And yet, there was *something* I could do. This stranger's words had to be a rouse. A game to trick me into leaving my guard down before the death blow came.

He jumped off the ledge and landed in the pond's shallow waters. From there, he walked barefoot along the edge. I waited for him to come for me again, but he paced back and forth and fixed his midnight black eyes on me. He wore nothing but trousers.

"Have you never noticed how you can smell things other people can't? The way certain animals avoid you?"

Sweat ran down his chest, drawing my eyes to his chiseled body.

I kept my mouth shut. He'd asked the right questions. I'd never shifted into another creature, but many folks, like the field hands living at the orange farm, depended on my intuition to sniff out tree rot and early blooms.

Farm animals didn't like me either. The farm's tabby scampered away whenever I drew near, and the chickens went into a frenzy when I walked past the coop. I assumed I had a strange scent.

My awkwardness carried over into courting, too. Not a single man came by the farm to ask about me, even when I dropped subtle hints of interest. At the fall festivals, after the long harvest, many gathered in town to celebrate with music and dancing. No one asked me to dance, and men averted their eyes as if my gaze would strike them dead.

"Maybe I am different, but that doesn't matter," I said firmly. "I need that rose."

He took a step forward. "How about a wager, then?"

My eyebrows rose. I'd never trust him.

"If you reach your boat safely, I'll let you go," he said. "But if you don't make it, you become my mate."

"This is your territory. You have a distinct advantage." I climbed down.

He turned his back to me, revealing a set of jagged scars along his right shoulder blade. I wondered how he got those. Maybe from the many gators around here. After running his hands through his black hair, he smiled. "My rose. My terms."

The man gave me another toothy grin before he continued. "I'm a fair man. I'll give you two minutes as a head start." In his hand laid the silver rose. My head whipped around to see the vacant ledge. How did he do that?

All of this seemed too good to be true. A trap waiting to be sprung. I took a step toward him, eager to snatch the flower. In a couple minutes, I'd reach my boat, then I'd head home. A simple plan.

I grabbed the rose and bolted out of the mangrove circle. The mud clung to my boots, making it difficult for me to run. I glanced over my shoulder a few times, not bothering to think about the ticking clock. He gave me two minutes. Without a watch, I didn't know how much time had passed.

When I finally found the rowboat where I'd left it, I paused after getting in. I kept seeing the man's defiant grin and dark eyes. His laughter carried on the wind from the east. What was wrong with me? All I had to do was escape. My hand trembled as I reached for an oar. I grabbed it. The notches on the worn wood bit into my palm. I could leave and try to save my father.

Or I could accept what seemed like the inevitable.

The boat shifted as another large body stepped on. It was the tiger. I thought I'd won. Or had the chase been for nothing? Was it all a test to see if I'd really leave?

I scurried backward and peered at the lethal cat. His nostrils flared as he sized up his prey. The tiger nearly stretched from the stern to the middle of my boat. Golden eyes absorbed my every move. With a single swipe of his massive claws, he'd slice me to ribbons. Yet, he waited patiently.

The choice to become his mate was mine.

I held my breath and placed the oar in the water, refusing to look at the hulking beast in the boat. Maybe he'd leave once he knew I planned to escape. The moment I pulled away from the shore, he jumped out of the boat and disappeared into the swamp.

The breath I'd held came out as a heavy sigh. He could've killed me. My grip tightened on the rose until the thorns punctured my palm like a bittersweet kiss. I'd truly won. But as I glided away, my gaze flitted to the mangroves in the distance. Vibrant leaves yellowed and curled while the trunks grayed from decay. The waters grew oily and blackened.

Part of me wanted to flee, yet a yearning I'd never experience before left me breathless. I'd only known this man for a short period. I didn't even know his name. And what about my granny Adeline? The elderly woman had played a part in this as well. She likely sat on her rocking chair back home, knowing what would happen. She'd be grinning from ear-to-ear.

I had to decide.

Did I want him? Yes. Was I ready to face what would happen to Papa? I'd never be ready, but like Granny said, we all had to face goodbyes and new beginnings.

Before the plants around me died, I turned the rowboat around. As my oars sliced through the water, the drooping flowers stood at attention. I returned to the shore and stepped out of the boat. When I re-entered the circle of withering mangroves, the trees flared with life again, welcoming me to my new home.

The End

CRAFTED
WITH A
KISS

1

Pynnelope

"Pynn, you should eat some breakfast before you kill people on the battlefield this morning," my old squire, Grillo, grumbled while I cinched the straps on my gelding's saddle.

I eyed the steaming pot inside my tent. Overcooked oats churned near the rim. It didn't look *that* appetizing.

As he ladled another serving into a wooden bowl my eyebrows lowered. "When I told you I was hungry for the first time in my life, I was thinking more along the lines of honey cakes, strawberry crème, that kind of thing."

"Bah!" He made a rude noise and rubbed the bald spot on the back of his head. "You're practically a wee babe. You can barely chew anything and you're made of wood."

He did have a *point* there.

My cunning squire opened his mouth with another

retort, but I mounted my horse and bounded away before he could hobble over and offer me his bubbling concoction.

The Unaro Kingdom's army camp swarmed and writhed around me, getting into position for our final push today. If I could smile, I'd do so. My heart might not beat, but anticipation seeped through the tiny joints here and there in my body.

I had two tasks today: Prevent a war and take the next step toward becoming human.

Autumn was the perfect time of the year for a battle. Winter left ice inside my wooden joints and summer made me expand in strange ways.

The men parted for me to enter the fray. Countless rows of archers filled the rear.

"Give 'em hell!" one archer yelled.

"The Wooden Demon!" the boisterous ones cheered.

For the longest time, I had no name. I was no one until I'd arrived in Unaro a few years ago. Recalling the past gave me this strange emptiness I couldn't explain. This feeling wasn't hunger, but something far deeper. Not so long ago, between walnut and cedar trees on a windy prairie field as wide as this one, the King of Unaro had been hunting with his sons and discovered me lying there. I liked to imagine I was a project a carpenter had cast aside during a lonely winter. With loving hands he'd given me a detailed face, arms, legs, and features that Grillo had said were womanly.

I'd seen my reflection in the river. I begged to differ on that one.

Pretty much my maker had abandoned me like forgotten firewood.

"I almost burned you on that brisk spring day," the wizen king said to me a few years ago. *"You were partially covered in dirt. Yet, I didn't care much for the deer hunt and*

wanted to be alone. Perhaps that's why I'd been drawn to you." He shrugged at the time in a manner to show he didn't care whether I lived or died. Only that I served. *"You were lucky my signet medallion was loose that day...Even luckier that it fell close to you."*

Through a dash of magic I didn't understand, the signet had ended up between my collarbones and I'd gotten up. Voiceless. Not breathing. But something had sparked inside of me. I trailed after the king and his party all the way back to the Unaro stronghold. To this very day I still followed him on his grand mission: to establish peace among the four warring kingdoms in the land of Veil.

My thoughts settled back to the task at hand, the battle this morning. The cavalry was easier to ride between. Their formation wasn't as tight—yet they were far quieter and solemn than the archers. Most of them kept their eyes ahead. As if they were waiting for the fight to truly begin.

One gangly soldier glared at me. Hunger for spilled blood glistened in his eyes. Yes, it was my fault that the sheathed sword on his hip hadn't seen blood in a long time. Two other kingdoms had fallen beneath my feet. Their champions had ridden onto a field like this one and fought a good fight, but they'd surrendered. Even a few jokesters had wanted a piece of me. Once a lumberjack, carrying a rusty axe, had strode out onto the field and gestured rudely with his paltry man-parts.

I kicked his hairy arse up and down the field, too.

Every single victory yielded an irresistible reward. When a kingdom was taken, the ruling family surrendered their throne and their family signet. My king brought peace to their lands and I got my reward: another jewel. The first army, the Andeans in the southern lands, gave me an amethyst. From that day forward I could speak. Forty days later, the Crasoon people of the north fell to their knees and ended the squabbles among their aristocrats. Their champion surrendered quickly and the opal signet their queen gave me had been special. Pangs of hunger finally hit my silent gut.

I was one step closer to being human.

A year later, we were at the Daquer border for my final fight. The end was near. By dusk my heart may beat and I might breathe. Would feeling air through my chest mean I was truly alive? I was willing to do anything at this point to be more than Pynn the Wooden Demon. I still didn't fear pain, but I longed to know the feeling. At this point, battle axes left me tired. Arrows didn't bother me either. Fire used to leave me quivering in fear. Not anymore.

How can you fear death when you truly don't understand what it means to be alive?

Today I felt something I hadn't felt before. Anticipation in my stomach. Was that what every soldier hungered for? This strange feeling?

Soon enough, I reached the edge of the Unaro front. Our commanding officer gave me a progress report. He wasn't the only one who wanted to see me.

A few squeaky chirps filled the air and then a familiar friend appeared. A tiny, black-and-white bird, about the size of my hand, swooped down from the overcast sky. Its long beak aimed for my head. In the past I'd had to run from the little bastard.

"Let me take care of it." An archer stepped forward to take aim.

My hand rose. "Leave it be. He's an *old* friend."

Friend was a loose term. I had a few chip marks from where that woodpecker had tried to get a piece of me. A few infantrymen smothered a laugh or two. This wasn't the first time a laugh had been made at my expense. Either way, the bird deserved to live as much as I did. I hated to kill people and I still wouldn't unless absolutely necessary.

A cavalryman followed me to my final position, using his sword to drive the poor animal away. If I could laugh, I would. Somehow, for some unknown reason, that animal always seemed to find me wherever I went. As I had been made from the very wood which should have been his home.

Across the field I searched for the Daquer army champion. There were thousands of men. An army that rivaled Unaro's. They had far more archers and men-at-arms. Their catapults didn't look as old and well worn as ours.

They might have an advantage, but the Old Law was still valid in the four kingdoms. Trial by champion was granted to those who asked for it seven days before battle.

A horn sounded from the Daquer line. Not far from me, our reply came. Both positions were ready. A few miles away, I spotted him. He dressed in a manner unlike the other champions. Others had worn full armor, but this one rode to the middle of the field on a beautiful white stallion wearing nothing more than leather armor.

I clicked and nudged my gelding forward.

We met in the middle. The closer and closer he got, I expected him to be like the others. The first champion had worn full armor and I'd never seen his face. But this one was bold. He had a sharp glint to his black eyes and shoulder-length hair. He stared at me, his dark gaze unyielding—until he was a few horse-lengths away. Then his hardened expression changed to something I couldn't place. The scar marring his face from the middle of his forehead to his cheekbones softened. His frown became less menacing. Maybe he was assessing me for weaknesses.

I waited. This could go two ways. Either he rode hard to full on attack me, or he'd let me begin this little dance. I preferred when my opponent wanted to get up close and personal.

He spoke first, surprising me. "You're not what I expected. At all. Do you re—"

I chuckled. A *clack-clack* noise from my voice box. "Did you expect a lady in a dress, perhaps?"

"It's been said the Wooden Demon had obsidian horns and a spear for its right hand." His gaze swept over me. "I'd say...you're taller than most men."

"The same could be said for you," I replied. "Maybe..."

Behind me, the Unaro army stomped their feet. The deafening clank of the cavalry hitting their shields vibrated along my arms.

In a fight between champions there were no rules. Either submission or death. I preferred the former.

"If you submit now," he offered softly, "this will end quickly and you won't be harmed."

My entire body shook with laughter. I nudged my gelding toward him for good measure. Time to fight. We slowly began to circle each other. This should be an interesting fight. We were evenly matched. Height for height, arm length for arm length. As to how well he wielded his weapon, I'd soon see.

Remember your swordmaster's training, I reminded myself.

"*If you can see their eyes, watch them,*" my swordmaster would say in an offhand manner. "*The weak ones reveal everything.*"

I unsheathed my long sword, and we closed the distance. His dark eyes focused on mine. Waiting for a reaction. Waiting for me to make the first move. So be it. I was never one to deny a man his defeat.

I charged and swung hard at him, ready to block with my shield when my side became vulnerable. The Daquer champion parried the blow with ease. And so our battle began. He was fierce with his swings, but I managed to maneuver my horse and dodge. The joints along my limbs bent at all sorts of angles. Backwards, forwards. My maker had likely crafted me to sit all day in a seat, but with such exquisite care to my construction, he'd unknowingly made me a war machine.

But I wasn't perfect. Through speed and an uncanny nimbleness, he clipped me twice in the arms. Not a full blow though, but rough nicks here and there.

Grillo, my swordmaster and squire, had taught me well over the years, but no technique could make me jump higher or run faster. I had to use my range of motion to my advantage and wait for my enemy to tire. Like right now— he approached me hard on his stallion, but his swing was wide.

Seizing the moment, I jumped off my horse and slammed into him, shoulder to chin, as hard as I could, and it was all I could do not to give a triumphant *clack-clack* as he tumbled back and we fell into the muddy dirt. He recovered quickly and stumbled back up to his feet despite rubbing the back of his head.

His breath came out in gasps. Had I finally tired him out?

Then he came at me again, grabbing my outstretched right arm. Like an agile dancer, he twisted faster than I expected and forced my arm back until it couldn't bend any further.

Shock shuddered through me. *How did he know my arm couldn't bend back that far?*

Before I could turn to strike him, he had me face down in the dirt with his heavy foot on the middle of my back. The Daquer army roared with pleasure.

Those bastards shouted all sorts of lively names. "Burn the Wooden Bitch!"

"Give us its arm!" another cried.

I finally managed to turn my head toward the Daquer line. Waited for the champion's final strike. What did come though was my release. The weight over my body was lifted. Only to be held again from weighted nets.

I sank into the mud. Again. Trapped like an animal.

Fiery, bright lights raced across the sky. More arrows from the Daquer line flew toward the Unaro army. The roar of catapults shook the ground. My mouth dropped as endless rows of men-at-arms charged.

"No..." the voice box in my throat murmured.

From my position on the ground, I had no choice but to watch my enemies sweep over the Unaro force like black ants overwhelming their latest kill.

I had been deceived from the very start. They had never planned to honor the Old Law.

2

Pynnelope

Not once in my life had I slept. I envied that in the living. Grillo had once told me fondly of waking up at dawn and feeling refreshed. Feeling the warmth of the dawn on your face and the joy at what was to come. My squire never took another wife after his first one died in childbirth and I wondered why he never did.

"Another woman? Bah! I have memories to keep me warm at night," he used to say. *"Dreams are what I look forward to when I'm awake."*

I cannot dream, and therefore my past torments me.

Being awake during the battle meant I had to watch my brethren be slaughtered as they fled. Even up to the point where I was dragged away across muddy fields and streams until I reached the enemy's castle. None of these memories could be dulled with sleep. What I wouldn't give for yesterday's events to be the ash dying in the stone fireplace near my feet.

All the while, the final signet I needed tugged away at me. It was close. Not in the same room, but close enough to tease me with the promise of life. I could practically taste the breath that would some day flutter through my body.

Now I lay wrapped in iron chains in someone's private quarters. There wasn't much to the place—a narrow bed, table, and a storage chest. The only light in the room came from the fireplace and a tall window along the wall. As to who the room's owner was, I didn't know yet. A soldier came by every couple of hours to tend to the fire, perhaps keep the flames high as a threat.

"Use a leg if you run out of wood," I'd murmured once.

After a while, I guessed they got tired of my ramblings so they tried to cover my mouth. A rather interesting feat since I couldn't breathe. Yet.

The morning sun rose high enough in the sky to cast a ray from the high window onto my prone body. Silence became my new companion. I almost wished that bird had found me by now. The monotony ended with the next guard, a new one I hadn't seen yet, who roughly yanked me up by the neck to examine me.

"Only foul spirits could be behind all this," he declared as his free hand raked down my cheek. He followed the line of my chin until he came to my mouth. With his fingertips, he tried to pry my small mouth open.

"Show me, Demon!" he spat. "I want to see what spirits are trapped in there."

The door opened.

"What do you think you're doing?" The Daquer champion, my betrayer, advanced across the room.

"Kristos, it was trying to escape," the guard began.

"It's a she," he replied darkly. "If she could escape, she would've done it already."

The guard's confident smirk turned into a straight line. "It's a demon. Who knows what it can do."

"Get out." The champion stood a foot taller than the guard. The poor man tried to stare back, but cowered under Kristos's glare. "Come in here again. Try it. I'll tear a hole through you so wide a caravan will be able to drive through it."

The guard managed a nod and left in a hurry. Once the guard was gone though, the man the guard called Kristos, unsheathed his sword.

My gaze shifted to the weapon in his hand. It was a beautiful blade, its edge smooth as if recently sharpened. He leaned down and I waited for death again. For the sleep I'd always been denied. Would I quickly die from a killing blow and sleep forever?

Instead of the sword's sharp edge, his hand checked my chains. His touch was soft, yet firm.

"Were you harmed?" he asked.

I shook my head, aghast at this kind treatment.

"Your arms..." He examined me closer than I'd prefer. "That angle doesn't look good. Does it hurt?"

"No." Hearing his deep, smooth voice made me not want to speak. My voice was hollow and awkward. Like a breeze fluttering down bamboo shoots.

"Good," he whispered. "You'll be chained until you tell me what I want to know."

Kristos

THE CREATURE LAY QUIETLY BEFORE me. It took everything in me to not ask a single question: *"Do you remember me?"*

My little *Drykola...*

I released the breath locked in my chest. Distant memories of her flooded me. Two years, four days, and a half-day of carving, constructing, and polishing. The very thing I'd crafted with my two hands was moving and talking. Some force had changed it, giving it the life I'd longed for after my fiancée Elisia died.

Briefly, I glanced away. Looking at its—her face—had been hard the moment we met on the battlefield. Tales of the legendary Wooden Demon had been unbelievable. There were no such things as monsters with horns or creatures with spears for hands. I never believed it. And yet, my creation, who had galloped onto the field with a gallant air, had held her mythical, wooden head high. Every feature I'd carved into her body was still there and my heart clenched. For the longest time, I thought I'd carried emptiness since I'd left her behind, but now I carried anger. Enough anger to conquer anyone in King Jeffren's path.

Even if I closed my eyes, I still saw the likeness of Elisia's cherub-shaped face, her rounded cheeks and full lips on the creature before me. From Elisia's brown eyes to the dimples dotting her cheeks. I'd spent weeks chiseling curves that were undeniably female.

Three royal signets adorned her form. According to the guards, they wouldn't come off.

Her limbs were filthy and covered in dried mud and grass. I almost fetched a cloth, but I pulled her up instead. Now wasn't the time for kindness. It took some effort to lift her with the chains. Damn it, she was just as heavy as I remembered. She shifted to properly hold herself up. When she couldn't she slumped forward until she hit the table.

The need to help her made me pause, but I forced myself to sit down on the opposite side. *I had a job to do.* The Daquer signet in my pocket tugged forward again. Almost as if the king's medallion sought out her presence. A part of me wanted to outright give it to her, but that would leave me no leverage for what I had to do.

We sat there for a few hours. The wooden warrior didn't speak, nor did I. She never asked for water or food.

When the next guard came to tend to the fire, I got up to leave.

"Whatever you seek, I cannot give you." So she finally decided to speak.

I didn't want to look at her again, but I couldn't resist. She wasn't human, but there was something soft and feminine about the way her head tilted to the side. The pine varnish on her cheek reflected the light from outside.

For the next two days, she sat in the seat and didn't speak. Questions went unanswered, yet I refused to torture her.

On the third day, I finally got a real response. My attempts at politeness ended.

"We can sit here all day again, if you like," I began. "Or we can talk about what will happen if you don't cooperate."

No reply.

I continued. "I've heard you've served the Unaro army for nearly two years. That's long enough to learn a thing or two. Especially as a *tool* for your good-for-nothing king."

Her bound fists tightened. Good. My little *Drykola* was loyal.

"Did you know what he planned to do with the land he acquired after his so-called peace campaign?" I asked.

"You're a champion," she grated out. "You've probably done nothing more than lift a sword. As if you'd know what a farmer does with *his* land?"

What a beautiful voice she had. I never imagined such a thing.

I leaned forward and showed her my hands. Her gaze flicked to the evidence of my past labors. "He's a liar. And you nearly helped him succeed."

She didn't move as I continued. "If you tell us how to enter the Unaro stronghold and drive him out to face justice, you'll be doing everyone in the Veil a favor."

She made that *clack-clack* noise again. Her laugh. "Do the slaves in Daquer know justice?"

My jaw tightened. Under King Jeffren many of my family members had been enslaved until I had the means to free them.

"All life has value," she said. "In every kingdom I conquered, the slaves were set free. Every one." Her mouth didn't move, but I could've sworn she was smirking.

I was ready though. "How much land was given to the aristocrats versus the farmers? Maybe a parcel or two to the original owners?"

Wood ground against wood. Her anger leeched out.

Since talking wasn't working, I'd have to try other means. This back and forth was getting us nowhere—until I heard a strange noise. Like rocks tumbling in a bag.

"What's that?" I asked.

She glanced away. "I haven't eaten anything."

So she ate food? *How?* "If you're hungry, I can give you whatever you want for the information I need." I regretted my words after I said them, but I had no choice.

"I'm not that hungry." She trembled and feigned disinterest. Hunger wasn't something you could hide though. It was a feeling I had known all too well as a child.

I stood and fetched food at once. A small bowl of chicken broth and some bread from the kitchen.

At first, I tried to feed her at the table, but she couldn't sit up properly. Which meant I had to try other means. I untied the iron chains around her legs. Our gazes locked and an understanding passed between us. *Food and a bit of freedom for cooperation.*

Once she sat up correctly at the table, she accepted the broth I gave her without spilling a single drop. The only sound in the room was the scrape of the wooden spoon against her mouth. I hadn't felt such ease in so long. Almost as if I was feeding Elisia. I hid a self-satisfied smile.

Until I pushed a portion of bread into her tiny mouth. She awkwardly tried to chew. *Chomp. Chomp.* And failed.

"This is so embarrassing." Bits and pieces rained down on the floor.

"Do you have a name?" I asked as I served her more broth instead, trying to be as casual as possible. Calling her by the name I knew her as would throw both of us off kilter.

She paused as if considering whether she'd answer. "Why do you want to know?"

"Do you prefer prisoner, perhaps?" I shrugged and smiled. "Wooden Bitch..."

I caught a *clack-clack*. So I made her laugh again.

Finally, she spoke. "It's...Pynnelope."

"So she has a name." I placed the food on the table. "Did your maker give you that name?" There were so many things I wanted to know about her. What had she been doing all this time? Where had she learned to fight so well?

"I don't know who made me," she replied. "My squire

Grillo named me after his youngest daughter who'd passed away a long time ago. His Majesty never gave me a name. Even after he learned about my presence in Unaro." She paused as if deep in thought. "The time before I had a name seemed so long ago...at first, I had been the Thing. A strange Thing that walked and frightened people. No one gave me a place to stay until I'd found Grillo. He had served many knights, but his Majesty had never knighted him."

Her fists clenched and unclenched. "It made me so angry to see a swordmaster treated so poorly. A man like Grillo lived in an ill-kept hut outside the Unaro stronghold. And yet, he took me in and named me. Over time, he even taught me how to *fight*." Her voice rose. "How to *live*."

While she spoke with fervent passion about her life with Grillo, jealousy blossomed in my chest. If I would've kept her, she would've remained lifeless in my old carpenter shop, and yet, after abandoning her I was still to blame for what she'd experienced. "And what about the man who'd made you. Do you ever think of him?"

Her head cocked to the side in a coyish manner. "I used to daydream about the man who'd made me," she said. "I imagined he spent years making me and loved me more than he loved himself. Once he was done though, something horrible had happened. Maybe he was taking me somewhere and died along the way. I liked to believe he died while holding me. Or maybe that he had been dragged away—"

A knock sounded on the door and a soldier entered.

"His Majesty has summoned you to his private quarters," the man said.

I cursed under my breath. Such an order couldn't be denied.

"You'll have to excuse me." I considered how long I'd be

gone. King Jeffren didn't honor the Veil's Old Law, nor did he care for his soldiers either. "Will you be all right sitting there with your arms tied?"

Clack clack. "You could untie me, if you like?"

As much as I wanted to free my little *Drykola*, I couldn't.

I said, "I'll return soon, Pynnelope."

ONCE I ARRIVED in King Jeffren's vast, private chambers, he didn't waste time conveying his displeasure at my failure. "Why haven't you given me what I want, Kristos?"

I got down on one knee and lowered my head. All these movements were pretense. An act I played for a man who cared more for himself than his subjects. This fact was evident in the marble floors from Crasoon, the priceless artifacts adorning the walls to the Unaro slaves who served his every whim. King Jeffren, the absolute ruler of Daquer's five great cities, sat in the middle of it all, a burly man who had never lifted a finger to protect his borders.

"She is loyal to her king, your Majesty." I glanced to my left. There were familiar faces in this opulent chamber. My young squire and his younger sister stood with clasped hands and bowed heads next to Craven, the king's personal guard. Not good. My king had promised me he wouldn't touch them.

Anger pulsed through my fingertips. I forced my hands into fists.

King Jeffren made a rude noise and dabbed the side of his mouth with a scented scarf. The overwhelming lavender aroma did little to mask the king's foul body odor.

"I hired you for a reason, boy. I command and you do as

you're told." He sniffed noisily. "You've wasted a few days already and I've been far too lenient. The more time we give Unaro to regroup, the less time we have for a surprise attack." His Majesty's gaze flicked to his guard and that bastard snatched my squire by the back of the head. He easily raised the lad a few feet in the air. The boy squeaked. In two steps I advanced on them, but stopped cold as Craven raised his dagger to my squire's gut.

"Go ahead and take another step, Kristos." The man grinned, revealing browning teeth. "I've been waiting for you to fail so I can kill him."

The king had made me into someone I detested—a man without recourse but to obey.

King Jeffren slowly smiled. "You always had a soft spot for people. That is your weakness. Ever since I drew you into my ranks from that hovel you called a carpenter shop, I'd been waiting to use you for your *true* purpose. Destroying my enemies. And now that I have you, I plan to bleed you dry."

The king gestured to Craven and the guard dropped the boy.

I shuddered from the need to strike.

Elisia's words from so long ago rang through my darkened senses: *"After you return from Crasoon, we're leaving Daquer. No more fighting. No more death. I'm tired of seeing your bloodied hands."*

I wanted more blood on my hands. The king's blood. Ten strides separated us. Practically a canyon if I thought about it. Even if I got past Craven and tried to strike the king down, his slaves who feared his wrath would defend him with their lives.

"You have until midnight, Kristos," King Jeffren warned. "After that, I'll let Craven kill them both."

3

Kristos

In less than a day, two people may die due to my actions. And the very idea that I had to bend to King Jeffren's will made me want to crush him with my bare hands.

Either way, I had until dawn to force Pynnelope to do the unthinkable: betray the people who hadn't cast her aside like I did.

Her words bounced around my head as I stormed out of King Jeffren's quarters.

"I used to daydream about the man who'd made me," she'd said. *"I imagined he spent years making me and loved me more than he loved himself. Once he was done though, something horrible had happened. Maybe he was taking me somewhere and died along the way. I liked to believe he died while holding me. Or maybe that he had been dragged away..."*

But I had left her behind.

I wandered briefly, trying to gather my scattered thoughts. My journey finally brought me back to my quarters to face Pynnelope. She was where I'd left her, sitting at the table tied in chains.

Shame stirred in my stomach. Without a word, I picked her up and carried her outside. I refused to do this without at least letting her enjoy the feel of the sun on her face. Along the way no one bothered me. She was still a bound prisoner and I was her interrogator.

There were plenty of gardens tended by the king's master gardeners, but my feet took me past them to the one place I rarely ventured. Stone paths led us to a few cottages and an ancient courtyard. This new place left Pynnelope enthralled.

"This garden is beautiful..." I heard her whisper in my arms.

Daquer was a kingdom of conquerors, not artisans. This courtyard had once been laid with the utmost care, but bloodstains and scorch marks marred the circular stone center. Chrysanthemums and other autumn flowers had witnessed many awful things.

I placed Pynnelope on a stone bench and forced my mouth to move. "I didn't bring you here to show you this place, Pynnelope. There's something I have to tell you...I know the man who made you."

Slowly, her head turned from the gardens to face me.

"You'd been found in a cedar and walnut tree grove, yes?" I kept going. "About two feet deep under the ground?"

She glanced at her feet and then back to me. "I hadn't been *buried*. What makes you believe I had been?"

Knives coursed down the back of my throat. "Because I *put* you there."

For the longest time she stared at me.

"Many years ago, I eloped with a woman named Elisia," I began. "She was outspoken. Tall and beautiful. She fell in love with the Daquer King's swordmaster. Me. Over time, I obtained power. Villages without an allegiance bowed to the crown under my hand. Men without a leader followed me. According to the king, I grew too powerful and had to be reminded of my place." My throat began to dry. "After a short campaign to defend the border with the Crasoons, I returned to find Elisia missing and a burning pyre right here in this courtyard."

Pynnelope stiffened. "So he killed her...to spite you?"

"He took the only thing I loved as a clear message: my life and the people that I loved belonged to him." I picked up a rock and clenched it tight enough to hurt my palm. "I collected her ashes and left my post that very day. Time passed. When I grew tired of sitting still I took up my father's profession, carpentry. That first year had been hard. Too hard. I drank myself to oblivion. When oblivion wouldn't accept me, I traveled across Veil—until I came to a beautiful cedar and walnut tree grove. The trees grew tall and the wood was firm. Right then and there I resolved to use my skills to craft you, in remembrance of Elisia."

She didn't speak so I kept going.

"After I made you, I was so happy, but my pain ran too deep so I buried you in Unaros," I whispered.

She snorted and shook her head. "I guess I didn't make you happy enough." Her eyes flashed with venom.

"You gave me purpose, *Drykola*."

Her chin rose upon hearing that name. "Drykola?"

"That was what I'd named you. It means 'wood tree bird' in the ancient Daquer tongue. We had a family of them living in the wood I used." I wanted to touch the top of her head to comfort her, but stopped myself. "I should've let Elisia go and made you your own person."

I sighed. "The gods have given me an opportunity to fix my mistakes and do what I was meant to do." I loosened the chains around her torso. "And that means taking care of you and dealing with the hold my King has over me."

I pulled the Daquer signet medallion from my pocket. The diamond gleamed under the day's sunlight. "Would you forgive me if I gave you this?" I had to hold the signet tightly. Some unseen force connected them together. As if Pynnelope and the royal signets had once been one but something had pulled them apart. "You can take it and escape. I'll rescue my squire and hold them off as long as I can. Maybe someday we'll find each other again."

I brought the jewel closer to her. My grip never wavered. With only a few inches to spare, a miraculous thing happened.

My Little Bird took her first breath.

Pynnelope

MY FIRST BREATH. It was rather hard to describe. My solid chest expanded and contracted. Shook and sputtered. A relieved hum settled in my chest and I truly spoke my first words.

"So that's what flowers smell like," I whispered. My voice was pure. Smooth like water flowing along a brook.

Kristos placed the signet over my heart. Once he was satisfied with its placement, he tossed the chains into the flowerbeds and returned to me. "We shouldn't say good bye to each other so how about 'until I see you again'?"

He placed his warm hand on my cheek and stroked the wood along my chin. When he began to withdraw I placed my hand over his. Now that I'd found my maker, he'd never get rid of me. I'd always remember our turbulent past, but now I had to think of the future. "How about we settle for goodbye after I've set *you* free?"

His right eyebrow rose. "I want to see you walk away on my terms, *Drykola*."

My stomach fluttered. A strange, yet delightful sensation.

"I could get used to this breathing thing..." To distract myself, I tried to whistle a soft tune Grillo whistled in the mornings. My shrill noises sounded like a choking bird. "Ehh, I'll stick to breathing for a while."

I folded my arms and looked over his pensive, handsome face. His scar made him more endearing to me. Did he really think I *couldn't* help him?

"Are you going to run away soon?" he pressed.

I retrieved the chains from the flowerbed. He had no choice but to follow. "Have you fallen off your horse and hit your head too many times?"

He blew out a long breath, and I knew from that moment on we'd get along splendidly. "You were a lot more cooperative when you didn't talk back," he grumbled.

I snorted. "Grillo often said that."

He finally accepted the chains and re-tied them around my torso. Once that was done, we set out.

"So where are they keeping your squire?" I asked evenly.

"Craven's got them. He's the king's personal guard. His

Majesty wouldn't have tolerated their presence for long—which means Craven took them to his quarters."

"Does he live in the village outside the palace? That would make our escape much easier."

"You'll see," he said with a cold finality.

We headed back into the palace. From the inner halls of the Daquer stronghold, we ventured straight until we reached a forked path—one led upstairs, while another went down. The path downward was darker than I expected. Light barely touched the damp corners. Once we climbed down two flights, Kristos removed my bonds and handed me a dagger from the sheath on his hip.

"Is this all you got? A rusty toy?" I quipped.

He ignored me and kept going.

The castle's bowels held a silence that sunk deep into my limbs. Almost as if the mold along the walls would crawl into me and poison me from within. We'd walked quite far for a personal guard's quarters.

"Why doesn't he have a room near the king?" I asked.

"Privacy," he replied. "No one can hear him when he brings women down here."

I nodded. Nothing else needed to be said. I'd met men like Craven before and when I hit them, they screamed just as loudly as the people they beat.

At the end of the long hallway, a line of light wrapped around a door. Kristos slowed down. His heavy footsteps grew quiet. We reached the door and I waited.

Kristos rested his hand on his sword's hilt. Drew in a deep breath. Then another.

With a grunt, he kicked open the door. I stormed in behind him to find a musty, well-lit room. Three guards stood at a tiny table in the corner. Haggard-looking slave girls dressed in filthy shifts sat at their feet. One guard had a bottle of mead in his meaty fist while the others were in the middle of a card game. The whole place stank of abuse and torture.

Fury quaked through my limbs. The squire, an older boy who looked to be no more than fifteen years or so, lay in a bloody heap on the floor while his younger sister cowered before a burly man with shortly cropped red hair and ruddy brown eyes. That had to be Craven.

They were scum. All of them.

Were we too late?

"Take the children and leave, Pynnelope." Death trailed Kristos's words.

"Why should she leave?" Craven drawled. "If she stayed long enough to play, I'll find out what his Majesty needs to know."

Craven didn't wait for an answer. With a snarl, he advanced on Kristos, swinging his sword wide. Kristos pushed me to the side as he vaulted out of the way to avoid the wild swing. The sword whistled with each strike barely missing Kristos's head.

Meanwhile, now that their show had ended, the three guards withdrew their weapons and looked my way. The women at their feet screeched and scattered for safe places to hide.

And all he'd left me was a dagger.

Those were the kind of odds a girl like me enjoyed.

They came at me hard, but I was ready. It was amazing what your first meal and a few days rest could do.

I had them right where I wanted them until one of them caught me in my elbow joint. Instead of pain—which I'd never experienced—I caught a new feeling. Discomfort. My arm bent at the elbow incorrectly, but I ignored it. No broken limbs yet. I disarmed one of them and grabbed his sword. A rather nice one.

Now the Wooden Bitch could play properly, too.

They came at me again with curses on their lips and a foul odor in their wake. I took backward shuffling steps, avoiding chairs and scrambling slaves. Three against one should've left anyone fearful, but I considered this fight fairer than most. With ease I slammed my fist across one man's cheek leaving him crumpled on the floor, the next man I kicked into the far wall, and the third—well he dropped his sword and made a run for it.

Now that my opponents were handled, I hurried to check on the children. The boy was unconscious and his poor sister's wide eyes told me she'd seen far too much for someone her age. Not far from me Craven and Kristos fought. In such cramped quarters, Kristos excelled. He quickly disarmed his opponent and left Craven clutching a stump.

Kristos had cut Craven's hand off.

"C'mon. Kill me you, bastard!" Craven screamed.

"The hand you used to strike these children belongs to me now," was all he said as he picked up his squire while I beckoned the girl into my arms. We left and hurried back upstairs. Instead of heading back to the courtyard, Kristos led us to the stables. Twilight greeted us.

"How will we escape?" I asked him. There were too many Daquer sentries.

"There's a guard post down the road from the courtyard we visited earlier." The dark look on his face spoke volumes. "It's heavily guarded, but it's the only chance we have."

By the time we stole two horses, the palace grounds had become a hive of activity. Soldiers were everywhere. Kristos placed the boy in front of me, while the girl clutched me from behind. Three riders to one horse would slow us down, but we managed to ride hard to reach the courtyard. I didn't look back. My charges didn't either. The boy was far too injured to care.

Far ahead of us, I could see bright torch lights. We'd made it to the guard post Kristos had warned me about.

Kristos looked my way. "Save them, Pynn. Don't stop. No matter what happens."

The serious look on his face bothered me. What did he plan to do? I opened my mouth to speak, but he urged his mare to run faster. Soon enough he rode ahead toward the lights. My heart, which now beat so vigorously in my chest, felt like it was crawling up my throat. Everything was happening too fast.

Kristos pulled his sword from his scabbard. The guards did the same. I almost closed my eyes as he crashed into them, bowling them over. I didn't get a chance to see much more. We safely made it past the guard post. It was all downhill from here to the dark-blue river separating the highlands from the mountains. I couldn't see him anymore, but I kept going.

"Save them, Pynn. Don't stop," he'd said. *"No matter what happens."*

The minute I heard the thunderous clop of my horse's hooves hitting the bridge, I released the breath trapped in my chest. As long as Kristos wasn't far behind me, I'd have everything I'd wanted. A new life and the man I'd dreamt of. The world was mine to conquer.

Something sharp hit my back. One moment I was on the horse, and in the next, I was flung into the air.

On the day I drew in my first breath I flew, too.

I landed on the bridge's muddy banks. From there I plopped into the river.

"No!" Someone called for me, but they seemed far away.

I tried to fight against the current, but my limbs were useless. All the power that had carried me through countless fights and battles was gone. I couldn't catch my breath. My limbs trembled uncontrollably. An icy feeling—like a bucket of winter rainwater—drenched me. The fingers on my good arm reached and brushed against an arrow. An arrow that had pierced King Unaro's signet medallion.

No, this wasn't fair.

Instead of sinking, I was carried downriver until long branches along the banks caught my legs. Murky water filled my mouth. I choked. I sputtered. I tried to breathe over and over again, but couldn't.

Death knocked on my door.

A pair of warm hands reached for me. Then a man's strong arm held my head above water while he dragged me to the riverbank. Once there, I knew the end was coming. In the twilight I couldn't see much, just shadows along my rescuer's worried face. Instead of joy, sorrow drew wrinkles along his handsome face.

"Kristos..." I could barely speak.

He cupped my cheeks and searched along my wound as if he could fix what was irreparable.

"Is the Lady gonna be okay?" the little girl asked from behind him.

Lady. She'd called me a lady.

I wasn't going to be okay. Those signets had made me real. Without them, I'd become nothing again.

"Kristos." My vision grew dark along the edges. "You can let me go... for real this time..."

Kristos

SHE LOOKED AT ME. I looked at her.

Then my creation breathed no more.

The young girl whimpered, and then began to wail.

I touched Pynnelope's chest, almost willing her to move. "Don't do this, Pynn...I'm not burying you again," I hissed.

The arrow came out after a few tugs, but she still didn't move. The diamond signet was broken. I leaned in and listened to her chest. Nothing. Then I tried again and caught it. A strange sound. A *click click click* noise. Was there still a spark of life within her?

I leaned over her face. Searching. Hoping. I didn't know what to do. I'd lost my chance all those years ago to untie Elisia from that post and save her from King Jeffren's wrath. Right now, Pynnelope was here and like everything I loved, she was being taken away. I drew her close to me, trying to draw my warmth into her cold body. She wasn't a machine. She was alive and I'd fight until my last breath to save her.

"You're not leaving me that easily." I pressed my lips against hers and blew. Her chest expanded. I tried again, this time my tears wetting her rounded cheeks.

When Pynn blinked, I couldn't believe it. That had never happened before.

She blinked!

My fingers brushed against her eyelids. Her body was still wood—and yet—she breathed and a heart beat inside her chest. I held something precious and miraculous in my arms.

"Did I die?" she finally whispered.

"Not yet, you haven't." I rested my chin on the top of

her head. "There will be no more burials. No more fighting. Just you and me, *Drykola*."

"So I'm alive?" she asked.

"To me you are." I kissed her again, lingering long enough to feel the smooth curve of her lips. Every exhale she made felt like the flutter of a butterfly's wings. I was soaking wet and chilled to the bone, but I'd never felt so content.

For hours we walked south along the riverbank until the Daquer army abandoned pursuit. We didn't have much, but we had each other.

"Should we set up, camp, sir?" my squire asked. "It's rather late." The young man was bruised, but smiling.

All this time I'd carried Pynnelope. She stirred as I placed her on the ground. My squire limped about to gather firewood.

"Where are we?" Her eyelids drooped.

I brushed my fingertips along her eyelids to force them shut. "Safe. In the morning, we'll go south to Andea and keep walking until we find a new home."

She refused to close her eyes. "All of us?"

I nodded. "Yes, all of us."

Finally, she closed her eyes and a heavenly sigh escaped from her lips. "I could never dream of anything better."

The End

About the Author

Shawntelle Madison is a Web developer who loves to weave words as well as code. She'd be reluctant to admit it, but if pressed, she'd say that she covets and collects source code. After losing her first summer job detasseling corn, Madison performed various jobs, from fast-food clerk to grunt programmer to university webmaster. Writing eccentric characters is her favorite job of all. On any given day when she's not surgically attached to her computer, she can be found watching cheesy horror movies or the latest action-packed anime. Shawntelle Madison lives in Missouri with her husband and children.